PRAISE FOR *A DOG'S HEAD*

In a modest way the author is working in the tradition of "Candide" and "Gulliver's Travels." The experiences of his hero enable M. Dutourd to register—lightly and divertingly—a ferocious commentary on the conduct of the human race. . . . M. Dutourd is a fine craftsman, whose work has the classic virtues of brevity, lucidity and concentration.
—Charles J. Rolo, *New York Times Book Review*

A Dog's Head is one of the most curious, most beautifully conceived and written fantasies you've ever come across. It is also a tale well worth speculating about, as you will find yourself doing throughout the book and after you have finished it.
—J. H. Jackson, *San Francisco Chronicle*

A tiny masterpiece in the French classical tradition. . . . It is a drama in miniature, the kind of thing that the French do superlatively well, stylish, elegant, and witty, and told with an apparent lightheartedness that points to rather than obscures the hero's essential tragedy.
—P. L. Travers, *New York Herald Tribune*

M. Dutourd is a satirist of the first rank. . . . One can go along with the fun without worrying about its implications, just as one can enjoy "Candide" as a burlesque picaresque novel without giving much thought to Voltaire's case against Rousseau's ideas. . . . It is easy to let the whole thing go with a burst of laughter. But the edge of Dutourd's joke cuts much deeper into man's relation with dogs.
—Anthony West, *The New Yorker*

A Dog's Head

A NOVEL

Jean Dutourd

TRANSLATED BY
Robin Chancellor

*With a new Preface by the author and
a new Foreword by Wendy Doniger*

THE UNIVERSITY OF CHICAGO PRESS
Chicago and London

The translator wishes to thank the Baroness Budberg for her generous criticism and advice.

The University of Chicago Press, Chicago 60637
The University of Chicago Press, Ltd., London

Copyright © 1951, 1998 by Jean Dutourd
English translation of Preface © 1998 by The University of Chicago
Foreword © 1998 by Wendy Doniger

All rights reserved. Originally published in Paris in 1951
under the title *Une tête de chien* © Editions Gallimard, 1950.
English translation by Robin Chancellor originally published by
Simon & Schuster, Inc., in 1953.
University of Chicago Press Edition 1998
Printed in the United States of America
03 02 01 00 99 98   6 5 4 3 2 1

Library of Congress Cataloging-in-Publication Data

Dutourd, Jean, 1920–
      [Tête de chien. English]
      A dog's head / Jean Dutourd ; translated by Robin
      Chancellor ; with a new preface by the author and a
      new foreword by Wendy Doniger
            p.   cm.
      ISBN 0-226-17492-1 (paperback : alk. paper)
      I. Chancellor, Robin. II. Title.
PQ2607.U865T413   1998
843'.914—dc21   97-51257
                                                          CIP

∞ The paper used in this publication meets the minimum
requirements of the American National Standard for Information Sciences—Permanence of Paper for Printed Library
Materials, ANSI Z39.48-1992.

Contents

Foreword

Wendy Doniger

WARNING: The following material is not suitable for children. Perhaps these words should be posted on the front page of this book, like the disclaimers before "adult" (i.e., infantile) television programs. *A Dog's Head* has the heady feeling of fantasy and suspended disbelief of a children's book. *The New York Herald Tribune*, in 1953, actually got a writer of children's books to review it: P. L. Travers, inventor of Mary Poppins (she called it "a tiny masterpiece in the French classical tradition . . . told with an apparent lightheartedness that points to rather than obscures the hero's essential tragedy"). At first glance, Jean Dutourd's book appears to grow out of the long tradition of books that, like *Alice in Wonderland*, both are and are not for children, resorted to by authors who wish to write lightly about subjects they fear may be too heavy to treat in adult literature without becoming maudlin. Such quasi-mythological narratives may also raise political and religious questions too dangerous, or too stark, to propound outside the safe space created by children's books. C. S. Lewis chose this genre for his great Narnian epic of Platonic/Catholic theology and mythology; he said in *The Lion, the Witch, and the Wardrobe* that the proper reason for writing a children's story is that "a children's story is the best art form for something you have to say." And Jean Dutourd certainly has something to say.

But this is no Gallic *Mary Poppins*. To begin with, it is not about cuddly anthropomorphic animals, like the Beatrix Potter gang (except, perhaps, for Squirrel Nutkin, a truly sinister theological character) or, more specifically, the upper-class British dogs in smoking jackets in Christopher Morley's whimsical *Where the Blue Begins*. There is whimsy here all right, but it is laced not only with irony (the usual companion of whimsy) but with bitterness. This is a book about a crossbreed, a half-caste creature. The dog-headed hero, Edmond Du Chaillu, encounters the sorts of social embarrassments suffered by all the fictional animals who have been subjected to what the anthropologist

Mary Douglas (in *Purity and Danger*) has taught us to call a category error—from Hans Christian Andersen's Ugly Duckling (who really is a swan) through Bernard Pomerance's *The Elephant Man* and Dick King-Smith's *Babe* (a pig who thinks he is a sheepdog).

Edmond is torn between his human desire to please his entirely human parents and his wish to carry a newspaper in his mouth or, always, to hang out with dogs. His dogginess is conceived in such realistic and delightfully observed detail that one can readily believe that a man might be born with a dog's head. But how was he born that way? The novel hints at the medieval idea of maternal imprinting: if a woman, at the moment of conception, thinks of a man other than her husband, she will give birth to a child who resembles the object of her fantasy. In *A Dog's Head*, Edmond's father asks his wife, "Did you think of a dog while you were pregnant?" "Never!" she replies, "Not once!" And then he asks, "in a still more broken voice," "And . . . before?" "Before?" she asks in surprise. . . . Christopher Robin, go to bed; the grownups want to talk.

This is a very funny, very serious book by a very funny, very serious man. Born in 1920, Jean Dutourd studied philosophy at the Sorbonne, was called up in 1940, and was taken prisoner soon afterward.

He escaped by jumping off the train on his way to Germany, and joined the Resistance. In 1943 he was caught by the Gestapo and sentenced to death, but again he escaped and resumed his underground activities. He is a man of action, and a man of parts; at one time he was fencing champion of Paris. His sense of humor was publicly established in 1950, when he wrote a guide to seduction, called *Le Petit Don Juan*, which bends the genre of children's books even as *A Dog's Head* flirts with it. *Le Petit Don Juan*, modeled on handbooks like "The Little Beekeeper" or "The Little Flower Gardener," also embodies a hilarious parody of Simone de Beauvoir's *The Second Sex*.

No, *A Dog's Head* is not for children, and not just because it toys throughout with the idea of bestiality. Its lineage is mythological, from the ancient tradition of *Beauty and the Beast*, more specifically the mythology of people with dog's heads who live on the margins of "our" world, a mythology recently and brilliantly illuminated by David Gordon White in *Myths of the Dog-Man* (Chicago, 1991). Dutourd's book is about that most postmodern of topics, Otherness. When *A Dog's Head* was first published in English in 1953, the *New York Times Book Review* and *Time* likened it to Voltaire's *Candide* and Jonathan Swift's *Gulliver's*

Travels; the *Saturday Review* also thought of Swift, and *The New Yorker* cited Voltaire but also, more tellingly, George Orwell's *Animal Farm*. Since 1953, however, a new genre has become prominent in which, I think, this book is more properly situated and which in many ways it anticipates: magical realism. This is the tradition of Borges and Fuentes and Isabelle Allende and Salman Rushdie, but also of Angela Carter, who retold fairy tales—including *Beauty and the Beast*—for a modern audience.

For *A Dog's Head* is no piece of animated ideology, any more than *Candide* or *Animal Farm*; it is a delicate, beautifully written book, hard to stop reading. One need not decipher the metaphor of a dog-headed man to enjoy the story; one can hold fast to the level of what Paul Ricoeur called a second naïveté and read it as a child might read it. On an even more literal level, one can also read it as, on the one hand, an indictment of the ways in which human beings have mistreated dogs (in the genre of *Black Beauty*, which was dubbed "The *Uncle Tom's Cabin* of the Horse") or, on the other hand, as an exploration of an extreme case of what Marjorie Garber has recently called *Dog-Love*, a fantasy on the reasons why humans love dogs. The fact that Edmond's dogs do not fawn on him as dogs are supposed to do threatens our conventional ideas not only about the normal behavior of dogs, but about the nature of human beings.

And if one chooses to read it as a human parable, *A Dog's Head* is a most touching and moving essay on marginalization and alienation, on the dilemma of a freak, which is to say anyone who has suffered from being ugly, or foreign, or racially other, or crippled, or deaf, or, I think, homosexual in a homophobic world. (The dog's natural wish to mate with dogs, when his parents and their world want him to marry a nice girl, is not very hard to decipher in this way.) Anthony West, in 1953, suggested that "what Edmond's friends say when they advise him against dog-fancying is exactly what they would say if they were telling him not to buy women." Almost a half a century later, I would say, rather, "not to buy men." When Edmond finally seems to find a woman who loves him, his gradual realization that she is a nut who thinks he's an enchanted prince waiting for her to disenchant him (which, again, one can read on the fairy tale level, or as a satire on women who hope to "reform" homosexuals) is convincing and very sad. The hero's descent into a life on the uneasy margins of the world, *entre chien et loup*, as the French say, is also convincing and more than sad: it is horrifying and tragic.

Preface

I was twenty-eight years old. One morning, looking at myself in the mirror, I realized I had
the head of a dog. You understand, of course,
that I was alone in perceiving this—no one around
commented on it—but it was undeniable: I no longer
looked as I had the night before.

When you have revelations like that, the only
way to cope is to write a book. So I wrote the
story of a man who has a dog's head—in other
words, my own story—hoping that when I had
reached the end of my tale I would have found
my own human head again: my nose, my eyebrows,
and especially my nice little ears. I did in fact
find all these, yet they were not exactly the nose
and ears I had had before. In this way I learned
that an artist metamorphoses with each newly

created work and becomes a different person after carrying a book to term.

A Dog's Head is my first novel, that is, the first work I wrote in the third person as if the hero were not me, although in part he was. The third person isn't easy to manage when you are young and very self-centered. Nevertheless, I succeeded, and that contributed greatly to my return to the human condition. Edmond Du Chaillu certainly was not me. All the less because I've never been the type to view life as tragic; I laugh at everything.

I still wonder why I gave my little novel such a cruel ending. No doubt my brain was full of the pessimism of youth. A story with a sad ending seemed to me more beautiful, more convincing, than a story that ended happily. And then, I had to, as it were, kill myself off—I had to change myself into a dog in order to be born again from my own ashes.

I wrote *A Dog's Head* in London, in the fog and the damp of an English-speaking city. Although I had written it in French, it seemed to me then the novel would be better understood by English-speaking than by French readers. That is just what happened. Britain and the United States found in *Une tête de chien* something familiar and gave it a warm welcome. *The New*

Yorker devoted three or four pages to it—an honor that could easily swell the head of a first-time novelist.

I have written many other novels since *Une tête de chien*, and probably better ones, but I have particularly fond memories of this story, as of a first love. Perhaps I learned my craft in writing it, since I sat down at my writing desk each morning like an artist in his studio, and that is the way a writer has to work.

Jean Dutourd

1997

A Dog's Head

ONE

WHEN she was told, as tactfully as could be, that she had just given birth to a child with a dog's head, Mme Du Chaillu fainted. After twenty years of sterility, it was a severe blow. M. Du Chaillu was, if possible, even more distraught. For fifteen minutes he seriously felt like killing his spouse, but one glance at her innocent face made him blush for his hideous suspicions. He contented himself with sighing: "My poor Henriette! We might have been spared this."

Mme Du Chaillu burst out sobbing.

"It's ghastly! How could it have happened? I
don't ever want to see it. Do you feel as miserable
as I do, Léon?"

M. Du Chaillu pressed Mme Du Chaillu's hand,
whereat she redoubled her tears. Blushing, he in-
quired in a choking voice: "Did you think of a
dog while you were pregnant?"

"Never!" cried Mme Du Chaillu. "Not once!"

"And . . . before?" murmured M. Du Chaillu,
in a still more broken voice.

"Before?" asked Mme Du Chaillu in surprise.

The child snuffled in its cradle. The head of a
puppy, frail and endearing, surmounted the swad-
dled body of this newborn human being. Its pink
muzzle, its unopened eyes and its soft fur wrung
from M. Du Chaillu his first tears.

"What will people say?" wondered Mme Du
Chaillu.

"Quite likely it'll die," said the midwife.

"We'll have no such luck," said M. Du Chaillu
sadly.

"Anyway, we can't call him Pierre," said Mme
Du Chaillu.

They called him Edmond. Mme Du Chaillu

could not bring herself to give him her breast, nor would the curé administer baptism.

"Let us wait till he talks," said the curé. "Suppose he has a dog's soul and barks? Ah, it is a great trial that the Lord has sent you, my friends. Prayer will help you to bear it."

Edmond's tongue was examined: it was flat. A real dog's tongue. He would bark, there was no doubt. The unhappy parents became desperate. Contrary to the curé's assurances, prayer brought them no solace; one would rather have said that it bored them. Then, at the age of six months, Edmond distinctly pronounced the word "papa," which gave ground for much rejoicing. He had the soul of a man!

In two years Edmond's head reached its definitive shape: it was a spaniel's, with long, flapping ears, wide, gaping jaws, and long hairs, masses of yellow and white hairs. For the rest, he was built like an ordinary human being. He was quite a charming child who talked, walked, filled his father's pipe and played with his mother's slippers. His parents could not help having some affection for him. One day, on his own initiative, he went to fetch the paper from the newsvendor and carried it home in his mouth.

"Little wretch!" cried M. Du Chaillu. "Aren't you ashamed of yourself?"

Edmond received a whipping which made him cry a great deal.

"Never try to repeat that joke," said M. Du Chaillu.

The first six years of Edmond's life slipped by much like the first six years of any small boy. Sometimes his mother cast him a look full of pity and sorrow, but he paid it no attention. His father did not like to see him in the proximity of dogs and was always chasing them away. Edmond would hear him say to his friends: "That child had a canine predestination."

Edmond understood that these words referred to him. Full of pride, he ran to the kitchen and confided to the cook: "Madeleine, I have a canine predestination. Papa said so."

"Run away to bed," replied the cook. "Don't bother me. I've my washing to do. Really! Your bite is worse than your bark!"

Edmond roared with laughter. He loved the girl's joviality.

4

The second whipping he was to remember was administered to him by his father one day when the latter caught him stroking a young poodle in the street. M. Du Chaillu, the chastiser, seemed to suffer more than Edmond, the chastised.

"Ah, Edmond," he said, panting, "what a difficult child you are! Hardly is my back turned before you're up to some dirty trick. Let me catch you at it again, and you'll see! My own son! Me, Léon Du Chaillu! In the middle of the street!"   .

Edmond could not comprehend his father's indignation. What could be reprehensible in stroking the nose of a playful poodle? But parental spankings have a strange power. The more Edmond was whacked on the behind, the more he felt covered with shame. He had indeed stroked a dog, and in the street, too. There must definitely be something very wrong with him to have felt neither embarrassment at the time nor any sense of guilt later.

"I confess I cannot understand you," declared M. Du Chaillu. "You are quite beyond me. What are children coming to nowadays? When I was a boy . . . Edmond, listen to me: I'm not an unkind man. I'm your father. I'm prepared to forgive anything, but not that. If I ever find you again

5

with a dog, I'll send you straight to a reformatory."

Edmond went without dinner and was sent to think things over in his room. He spent an hour regretting that such an amusing occupation as stroking a dog in the street should make his father so unhappy and earn him a beating. After which, he fell asleep and dreamed of savage dogs, which disturbed his slumbers.

M. Du Chaillu, for his part, said to his wife: "That child distresses me. He is unquestionably attracted by dogs, and we must avoid that at all costs. What can we do, Henriette? What can we do?"

Mme Du Chaillu was no less worried. "Do you really think it's bad for him to be with dogs?" she queried.

"Bad? No! Catastrophic! Besides, there's the question of morality. Understand me, Henriette. That boy has a canine predestination. We must do everything in our power to fight it. As far as I'm concerned, I shall be inflexible on that point."

It was decided not to speak of dogs before Edmond. When that couldn't be avoided, they would shower abuse on these animals. They would depict them as terrible, cruel, treacherous brutes, etc. Might it not even be a good thing to have Edmond bitten by some mangy cur so as to imprint their hatred in his flesh? This last suggestion, however, upset Mme Du Chaillu and was provisionally abandoned. Two china King Charles spaniels which adorned the mantelpiece were locked away in a cupboard, and a picture in the drawing room representing a St. Bernard rescuing a stray mountaineer was taken down—a rather second-rate painting, anyway. In three months dogs lost all their fascination for Edmond; he began to hate and fear them. They filled him with extraordinary repugnance. In order to frighten him, it was enough to say: "I'm going to fetch the dog . . ." and he would flee, shrieking. Nevertheless, his parents had not enough courage to carry their scheme through to its logical conclusion and inspire in Edmond a horror of himself as well. On the contrary, they did all they could to make him forget his spaniel's head. "I don't want my son to develop any complexes," declared M. Du Chaillu, who had heard talk of Freud. But in the long run it is rather difficult not to "develop complexes" when one has a dog's head. The friends of the family had all been cautioned. They behaved just as if Edmond had an ordinary child's face. They spoke to him of his chubby cheeks, they referred to his fur as hair, to his fangs as milk-teeth, and so on. An old aunt said to him one day, without meaning any harm: "Wipe your muzzle, it's covered with chocolate." The word "muzzle" made M. Du Chaillu jump several feet. He ordered the old lady to clear out and never come back.

Despite these admirable precautions and discretions, Edmond cherished no illusions as to his appearance. He examined himself ten times a day in the mirror. It must be admitted that his head did not displease him, nor was he at all self-conscious about it, as was believed. Once, when he had been particularly naughty, his mother in a fury cried: "You little monster!" He was quite unmoved by this. Wasn't this what all naughty children were called? His dog's head provided him with a thousand ways of amusing himself differently from other children. His range of games was far more extensive than theirs. For example, when his parents went out, he spent entrancing hours pretending to be a watchdog, until he even frightened himself. He barked more realistically than anyone. When, carried away by the excitement of the game, he chanced to bite somebody, this prank was straightway forgiven and concealed from M. Du Chaillu.

Edmond doted on the cook, Madeleine, a country girl accustomed to living with animals. She treated Edmond as he loved to be treated—with rough tenderness. When she was in a bad temper, she didn't hesitate to chase him out of the kitchen with a few hearty kicks. But she also had her good moods, and then she would take Edmond on her knee and scratch the crown of his head with such skill that she drew growls of delight from her little master. She would say: "There's my sweet little bowwow. There's my little pet. What beautiful ears he has, and what lovely big teeth! Oh, la la!"

Edmond had a wonderful time in Madeleine's arms—she was the only person who treated him without affectation. Usually these sessions ended with great lickings. Edmond would sweep his flat tongue over Madeleine's plump cheeks while she laughed and struggled against it.

"Wherever did I get such a dog?" she would gurgle. "It's not a dog, it's a little pig. Stop it! Now please, Master Edmond! Look! I'm getting all wet!"

Master Edmond would straighten his blue velvet

suit and lace collar, pull up his white socks and lick his dry chops. His heart pumped in his chest. Of course, M. Du Chaillu happened one day to witness one of these scenes. Madeleine was dismissed and Edmond reprimanded.

Mme Du Chaillu raised several objections when the time came for Edmond to be sent to school.

"The other boys will laugh at him," she said. "He'll be unhappy, poor child."

"He must learn to rub along with the outer world," replied M. Du Chaillu. "We can't always keep him at home with us, shut away from other men. One day he'll have to take to his own wings, and the sooner the better." In educational matters M. Du Chaillu always won the day. His wife soon submitted to his judgment; in fact, she had abdicated ever since Edmond was born. Bringing a child with a dog's head into the world had delivered a mortal blow to her character. Edmond, for his part, could not see why his parents should keep him shut up all his life. He greatly longed to take to his own wings, as his father put it, although this metaphor puzzled him. Standing before the mirror, he took his ears between finger and thumb, raised them horizontally and flapped them. He was surprised that this did not make him fly. The next morning he went off to school. He had been rigged up in a ridiculous manner: a Balaklava helmet, a cap pulled down to his eyes, dark glasses and a muffler wound high. He suffocated beneath all this, and, as soon as he entered the classroom, rid himself of these garments. The master then spoke up: "Boys, from now on you have a new comrade. As you can see, he has a dog's head. It is not his fault; he was born like that. Besides, I would draw your attention to the fact that his dog's head is a very handsome one indeed. Your classmate has a very fine dog's head. He has no reason to be ashamed of it, and you have no reason to tease him. I rely on your good manners, your charitable natures and your kind hearts never to persecute him."

Nothing could have been more prejudicial to Edmond than this homily. Though he was only six years old, he realized this perfectly. The longer the teacher droned on, the more he was seized with fear. He would gladly have dispensed with this friendly welcome, which singled him out for all eyes and all malice.

"If anyone tries to tease you," concluded the master in a severe tone, "you have only to tell me,

Du Chaillu, and he'll have me to reckon with. Is that clear?"

These final words were disastrous. To invite a schoolboy to tattle is to wreck his career forever. Edmond heard a murmur of censure ripple round the classroom, and shuddered. His stout little heart, however, bore no rancor against the master who was thus trying to protect him. He merely told himself that enemies are always cunning and allies always clumsy.

Edmond's schoolfellows swiftly divided themselves into three clans: the indifferent, the charitable and the cruel. Naturally, he professed the greatest admiration for these last, tried to win their friendship and join in their games, to which they only admitted him as a butt. Nevertheless, whatever the attitude adopted by the schoolboys—hostility, indifference or kindness—they did not behave with him as they did among themselves. They all had human heads, and Edmond had that of a dog. You cannot imagine how the fact of possessing a dog's head alters the disposition of those with whom one is called upon to live. The feelings they display toward you become immediately excessive and hence embarrassing. The good are too good, the indifferent too indifferent, the derisive too derisive. This lack of naturalness was experienced by Edmond for the first time at school, and it made him realize his inequality, so that it was at school that he first became conscious of this spaniel's head so oddly placed upon his shoulders.

His persecutors called him "Fido," "Rover," "Bonzo," "Puppydog" and "Rags." They asked him: "How are the old dogs at home?" "What! Haven't they put your collar on this morning?" "Who takes you out before breakfast, your mother or your father?" And a thousand other insulting things, or at least things intended as such, though they only sounded like amusing jokes to Edmond. On the other hand, the first time he was called not a girl but a bitch he grew angry. The real tortures were yet to come. He was forced to walk on all fours, to bark, and so on. He was tied by the neck to a post in the yard and nearly strangled himself. His nose was rubbed in dung. When he wanted to relieve himself, two boys silently followed him, seized hold of him and compelled him to fulfill his needs with one leg raised in the air. This gave rise to infinite hilarity. Nor were they unaware of his horror of dogs: thus they amused themselves by terrorizing him, crying, "Look out, Du Chaillu, there's a dog! He'll bite you . . . sic him . . . sic him . . . bite him!" Edmond, with loud howls, would rush to barricade himself in an empty study. In class, when a dog was mentioned, all heads would turn toward him and sniggers were let fly. The back bench, where half a dozen young bloods sat together, went "wuff, wuff," which made the teacher smile. La Fontaine's fable of "The Donkey and the Little Dog" raised gales of laughter for three days. Pedants whispered *"Cave canem"* in an undertone. This lasted until the day Edmond frightened his companions by biting one of them in the hand. It is true that he regretted this act much too precipitately, thus slightly diminishing his victory, but from that time on he was bullied much less and the school became accustomed to him.

Edmond proved to be an ordinary pupil, neither lazy nor brilliant, steering a comfortable middle course. At eight he was a senior, and joyfully participated in the bullying meted out to newcomers. He greeted them with a "Grrrrr . . ." which terrified them, and chased them round the yard with howls; in class he licked their ears, which made them shudder. He became a rowdy, and went on all fours, this time for his own pleasure, crawling between the forms and biting a calf here and there. In brief, he occupied a solid and honorable position in childish society. Finally, he learned to profit from the advantages of his physique. Reprimanded by the masters, he would whine: "I'm so unhappy! Oh, sir, if you had a dog's head like me!"

Later on he was to recall with shame these hypocritical laments which helped him to avoid detention.

M. Du Chaillu found that his son was improving and was well pleased with the effect other children seemed to have on him. Edmond never dreamed of confiding the secrets of his school life to his father. Wednesdays and Sundays had the same pattern for him as they have for everyone. Sometimes he went to the zoo to contemplate the monkeys, birds and lions; sometimes he was dragged off to a museum. Edmond dearly loved the zoo, where animals are deprived of liberty. M. Du Chaillu would sermonize him at length.

"Edmond," he would say, "you don't know how lucky you are. You are a being endowed with thought. You are clothed in fine suits which I buy for you at La Belle Jardinière and which cost me a great deal, I may add in passing. You walk erect on two legs, with your head raised toward the stars. You are a little Frenchman; that is to say, you belong to the most intelligent and glorious nation in the world. Later on, you will be a free man, conscious of your rights and faithful to your duties. Look at these unfortunate animals; they walk on four feet, their bodies are covered with fur, they are devoid of reason and they spend all their lives behind the bars of a cage. Don't you feel proud to be a man, Edmond?"

"But am I in fact a man?" Edmond asked himself. "There's no need to spin me any fairy tales. I have an animal's head. A dog's, I admit, and the dog is a domestic animal which is not shut up in a cage. But am I as much of a man and a Frenchman as Papa asserts?"

He knew, however, that his dog's head was a forbidden subject and carefully kept his reflections to himself. Wolves inspired him with a vague feeling of brotherhood which he dared not admit to himself and which seemed to him the peak of obscenity. He could not bear the gaze of the panther; he saw a reproach in that beast's eyes and imagined it thinking: "Why am I a prisoner and not he?"

This idea he found intolerable. At other times he congratulated himself that solid bars separated him from the animals, regarded them sadistically and enjoyed their sufferings, as a true sadist enjoys the sufferings of his fellow men.

At the War Museum there were other tortures. Edmond told himself that he would never be Napoleon and was inconsolable. He cursed the head which would always prevent him from becoming a leader of men. He regretted the Middle Ages: in those days men had their heads encased in helmets. Why wasn't he born eight hundred years earlier? He could have spent his life inside a helmet, with the following device on his shield: *El Desdichado*. How well it would have suited him to be Louis XIV's brother and wear an iron mask all his life, etc. Such are the daydreams of a boy with a dog's head.

Edmond sometimes went to spend his Wednesdays with a friend, for he had two or three who appreciated him and even rather admired him. These estimable boys had completely forgotten the dog's head of our hero and treated him as an ordinary little boy. Even their parents felt some affection for him; he roused their pity and served as a foil for their own offspring. M. Du Chaillu was most interested in these friendships, kept himself informed about them and followed every move, to Edmond's despair. One day, when the latter fell sick and missed school, one of his friends called on him. "Greetings, old Bonzo," he fondly said. M. Du Chaillu was standing in the doorway.

"Get out!" he cried. "I forbid you to address my son like that. You're a very rude little boy. I won't have you set foot in this house again. And you, Edmond, are not to see any more of this common creature."

Edmond flew into an indescribable rage. For the first time he ventured to think his father was a fool. He fervently hoped that his friend would be discreet about this incident at school. The friend was not discreet, and their friendship came to an end.

At eleven Edmond was confirmed. He was going through a phase of deep religiosity, had a passion for St. Francis of Assisi, and would willingly have exchanged his Eton jacket and patent-leather shoes for the hair shirt and sandals of the saint. He longed to lead an edifying existence surrounded by rocks and verdure. Hinds would come to feed from his hand. Birds would perch on his shoulders. Every stray, lost or unhappy dog would come to him, who had conquered his dislike of them, loved them and gave them shelter. He would load them with sweetmeats and caresses. At night they would share his anchorite's couch and keep him warm. A voluptuous tenderness overcame him. "How beautiful life would be," he thought, "if only I cared for dogs." Edmond was not, however, deeply pious. In a few months his mystic flights were over.

Edmond's mother had not, like M. Du Chaillu, adopted a system and a method of behavior toward her son. She alternated between joy and sorrow: joy at having a child and sorrow at seeing him with such a head. On the mantelpiece of her room she had displayed three photographs of Edmond. The first portrayed him at the age of three months: lying naked on his stomach, he made a pretty infant, plump and healthy; a broad smile was spread across his innocent little muzzle. The second picture showed him at five, astride a wooden pig on a merry-go-round: he was wearing short little trousers and the wind gently lifted his long ears. The third photograph was that of his first communion: with unctuously inclined head and armlet plainly showing, he stood with a missal in his hand. One day Mme Du Chaillu would seize these three pictures and kiss them passionately. Tears would stream from her eyes as she murmured: "My little Edmond . . . my little darling." The next day she would throw them angrily into a drawer, which she did not dare reopen for a fortnight. She behaved in the same way toward Edmond, now petting him without restraint, now displaying a peevish indifference of which she would swiftly repent. Ceaselessly she told herself: "It's not the child's fault if he has a spaniel's head. I'm a bad mother." She shuddered with disgust when Edmond, struggling with some grievance, took refuge in her arms and licked her, but she forced herself to kiss his eyes when he fell asleep. If one of his ears got crumpled under his head as he lay on his side, Mme Du Chaillu would gently raise him and smooth out the recalcitrant appendage. Lovingly she would tuck him up; then, alone in her room, suddenly flare up with rage at the thought of having such a child. "Oh, Heaven, what have I done," she groaned, "and why should my son have a dog's head? I did not deserve that!" She deplored her fate, keenly aware that she was the victim of an injustice which rendered her unjust toward her innocent child.

"Poor little fellow," she thought, "he is even more unhappy than I am. He is a dear boy and very good-natured. I wonder if his father is right to be so severe with him. Naturally, it's for his own good, but even so . . . I ought to be all the more gentle." These good resolutions lasted just the length of time it takes to describe them. Mme Du Chaillu could not bring herself to be consistent. Nothing could have disconcerted Edmond more, nothing could so embarrass him or estrange him further from his mother. At twelve he had lost all confidence in this extravagant, fantastic and unpredictable creature. He loved her only out of a sense of duty.

From the first to the sixth form Edmond led the ordinary life of a schoolboy, learning Latin, Greek and mathematics, and finding fun in dirty jokes and obscenity. He had a small gift for literature and handed in good French essays. His future preoccupied M. Du Chaillu, who did not want his son to be a failure. Apart from French, Edmond's reports were mediocre, and M. Du Chaillu would fly into a savage rage every three months. On one occasion he said: "You must be first in everything, my boy, for with your physique you will meet greater difficulties in life than other men. I don't see why I should conceal it from you any longer: you have a dog's head, Edmond. You are reaching an age when it is better for you to know the truth."

These words overwhelmed Edmond, not that he was ignorant of anything about himself at the age of fourteen but because his father had at last ceased to pretend that he had a human head. Edmond perceived in this that time was passing and that he had grown old or, if you prefer it, grown up. Revelations of this nature always cause an upheaval.

"Yes, Papa," he replied.

M. Du Chaillu, as if he were seeing his son for the first time, looked him up and down. This examination embarrassed Edmond deeply. He did not know what to do with his muzzle, his ears and his fur. He came near to regretting his father's former attitude. He felt naked before this man with whom he shared no familiarity. However, this only lasted for a second. Edmond returned at once to reality: M. Du Chaillu had at last agreed to face the situation. Such a sudden leap forward raised all kinds of hope in him. Without quite knowing why, but giving vent to a deep and constantly repressed desire, our hero suddenly asked: "I say, Papa, supposing we bought a dog?"

M. Du Chaillu's face clouded.

"A dog?"

"Yes," said Edmond, his confidence beginning to falter.

"No."

"Why?"

"You know very well why."

Edmond frankly did not know why his father so obstinately refused to acquire a dog. Unguardedly he sighed: "I should so much like to have a dog!"

M. Du Chaillu sniggered.

"Yes, I know. But don't count on me, my boy, to facilitate your unnatural proclivities. As long as I live no dog shall enter this house. Try to develop the tastes of your age. Good God, it's not difficult! Why, at your age, I collected stamps and played football: I wasn't interested in dogs. I want to turn you into a perfectly normal and healthy being. Your mother and I should quite adequately fulfill your need for affection."

"But a dog's not the same thing. . . ."

"Silence!" cried M. Du Chaillu. "Never mention it again."

Edmond lowered his head, overcome by a Christian's recoil before the sins of the flesh. The most horrible thing was that he couldn't fathom what it was all about. This interdict that his father placed on dogs aroused in him a perturbation of conscience similar to that which priests know so well how to awaken in adolescents. Edmond felt toward the canine species a mixture of fear and affection that was perfectly clear and pure. His father was an incomprehensible being, or else he perhaps discerned feelings in Edmond of which the latter was ignorant. Edmond hated him for causing him such embarrassment.

"Have you ever given any thought to your future?" asked M. Du Chaillu in a calmer voice.

"No, Papa," replied Edmond, bored beyond measure.

"With a head like yours, you can't expect to enter any profession you choose. We must find one which won't bring you into contact with many people. However, I don't want to influence you. Do you feel particularly interested in anything?"

"I don't know," murmured Edmond.

"You don't know! . . . Well, I don't know either, I must confess, though I've considered the problem from every angle. Whatever one's profession, it involves the company of one's fellow beings. I mean . . . of men. You will read for the bar. After that, we'll see."

Edmond, who still had four or five years ahead
of him before taking his School Certificate, found
this a futile idea.

When he reached the age of fifteen, he developed an irritating habit. He began to boast of his
successes with women. He painted himself in the
guise of a Don Juan, a Valmont or a Lovelace.
Adolescents are credulous creatures, and he had no
difficulty in persuading his fellow students that no
woman could resist him. Catholic in his tastes, he
ranged from housemaids to duchesses, not omitting
young girls. This was clearly nothing but boasting
and Edmond was as virginal as could be, but he
was shrewd, and his accounts breathed an air of
truth which was convincing. One day he made up
a story which deserves repeating. He was returning
home, his satchel under his arm, with no evil in-
tent, when what should he suddenly see but a
ravishing woman, blonde, elegant, about thirty
years old! She had a large greyhound on a leash,
walked with neat, rapid movements and one could
see, despite her long and narrow skirt, that she had
beautiful legs. Edmond, who was anything but
shy, accosted her. The unknown lady smiled, Edmond took her arm, and together they turned toward the superb flat which she occupied in the

Avenue du Bois de Boulogne, the sunny side. She dragged Edmond into her bedroom (description of the bedroom), closed the door and left the dog outside. While they were making love, the greyhound scratched and whined at the door. "She got pretty well worked up, that one," concluded Edmond.

"And the dog? What did you do with it?" somebody asked.

"The dog? Oh, I gave it a kick in the ribs and locked it up in the kitchen. That's the only way to treat the filthy things."

Sometimes Edmond even contrived to forget his dog's head for several days. When by chance he saw his reflection in a shop window, it didn't upset him at all. His ears, his muzzle, his whiskers and his lashless eyes were such a familiar spectacle, so often seen, that they caused him no pain. Certain people never grow accustomed to being crippled or disfigured and always suffer a terrible shock when they are suddenly made aware of their stump or their lupus. But it was not in Edmond's nature to mourn in vain. "I have a dog's head," he told himself. "Very well, I can do nothing about it. The matter is settled. The important thing is to make the best of this dog's head, which I am doing. Candidly, there are many more unfortunate people than I. Legless cripples, for example. By and large, my head is more of an asset to me than a liability. People don't expect to find such a lively intelligence and such knowledge behind a spaniel's whiskers."

Indeed, when he began to speak, his audience was rapidly captivated. Remarks which would have appeared lacking in interest if coming from normal young people were adorned with a special quality when they issued from his jaws. It was enough for him to say to someone: "Good morning, how are you?" for him at once to be rewarded with a look of delighted astonishment. After that, he made the most of his opportunity to hold forth about Leibnitz' *Monadology*, which he had not read, about the differential calculus, which he understood not at all, and Bach's "Goldberg Variations," which had bored him one evening at a concert.

Even so, one must not exaggerate. There were circumstances when he would have given a great deal not to have a dog's head; for instance, when he took his School Certificate. He had all the heedlessness of his sixteen years; he was late and began to run. Whenever he lost his breath or perspired, he reacted just like a dog, not like a man; that is to say, his tongue hung like a streamer from his mouth and he slobbered dreadfully. The examiner in Latin, all over whose Tacitus he dribbled, was so put off by this that he got no marks at all and had to take the subject again in October.

TWO

FOLLOWING his father's wishes, Edmond took a law degree, to which he added, on his own initiative, a degree in arts, since he had a taste for the classics. M. Du Chaillu experienced great happiness on seeing his son in possession of these documents. With parental blindness he cried: "That's the first successful attempt you've made to disguise your head, Edmond. You are no longer just a nobody with a dog's head, you are a gentleman. From now on you are Edmond Du Chaillu, graduate in law and arts, and that is that. I can confess now that for a long time I feared for you.

I saw you lazy, I saw you handicapped. I said to
myself: 'That poor boy will sink lower and lower.
He'll end up in a collection of freaks, between a
five-legged calf and a tattooed lady.' But today my
mind is at rest."

Edmond himself felt keenly that his dog's head
weighed much heavier in the scales than his diplomas. But enough of that! He was twenty; one
year of military service lay between him and real
life. In a year's time M. Du Chaillu would have
found him that ideal job which would not expose
him to any human contacts. At the recruiting office,
naked amidst two hundred naked men, Edmond
created an undeniably curious impression. Con-
scripts have simple and lewd souls. Their astonishment and the gibes they showered on him are easy
to imagine. Edmond knew only too well all that
could be said about his appearance, and so he replied good-naturedly to their offensive or obscene
remarks. This soon won him their esteem. When
his turn came to be examined, the major said: "The
army's no place for you, my friend. You should be
at a fair. With a head like that, I can discharge you
at once."

Edmond was annoyed. "Sir," he replied, "up to

now I have lived like a normal man. I have graduated in law and arts. I am very nimble and robust, in perfect health and filled with genuine patriotism. I should not be exempt from military service just because I have a dog's head."

"Very well," said the major. "I have warned you. It is your own wish. Passed fit for service!"

Having put on his clothes, Edmond rambled round the boulevards of the capital with some ten recruits who had taken him up. A cascade of tricolored ribbons fluttered from his buttonhole. He sang "The Gunner of Metz" and "The Girls of Camaret" at the top of his voice, and passers-by, moved by the occasion, looked at him and smiled. Edmond was as happy as a thief just released from prison.

At the Galliffet Barracks at Brioude (Haute Loire) he sang a different tune. The top sergeant never forgave him for his head. He regarded it to the end as a personal affront. When Edmond reported to him, he knitted his brows, and his mouth assumed a bitter twist.

"Ah-ha!" he barked. "I see. The young man's a humorist. He's trying to be smart. He doesn't want to be like the others. He wants to attract attention.

Very well! He shall learn what it is to be a Bohemian. To begin with, he will do me the pleasure of getting his head shaved."

So Edmond went to the barber. A cruel ordeal. There is nothing so pitiful as a shaven spaniel's head; it is thin and flaccid. Edmond was humiliated. Picture his poor head emerging from a khaki tunic, surmounted by a forage cap pointed at each end. It was of a stupefying absurdity. Providentially, the company to which Edmond was assigned was made up chiefly of young, rather dull-witted yokels, accustomed by their squalid lives not to be astonished by any physical peculiarity. Edmond had nothing to fear from them except a few rather ponderous jokes. They were comic enough themselves, with their nightcaps, their bottles of red wine which they made last for a whole week, and their rustic dialect.

The army is perhaps the only place left where a degree still commands a certain respect. In two days Edmond became "The Professor." This nickname gave him secret pleasure: the clodhoppers recognized him as their superior, in one way at least; and the N.C.O.s, despite the annoyance they felt at such an irregular soldier, could not refrain from

showing him just a little consideration. The top
sergeant alone remained indifferent to Edmond's
erudition. He regarded it rather as a tiresome cir-
cumstance and was not sparing of insults.

"The Professor will clean out the lats," he would
bawl. "After which, the Professor can wipe his
hands on his ugly big ears. Stand at . . . *ease!* At-
ten . . . *shun!* Eyes . . . *right!* Eyes . . . *front!*
Du Chaillu, keep those jaws shut. Christ almighty,
d'you want a bone? Quiet! Stick yer tongue in!
Now yer snout's stickin' out. Four days' confined-to-
barracks for arriving on parade in a carnival mask!
Get those ears in line, now! Du Chaillu! Stop wig-
glin' those ears or I'll make it eight days. Think
you're smart, do you, 'cause you've got a head like
nobody else's? I'll learn yer. I'll make a man of you.
I've broken in tougher bastards than you. You'll get
sick of the game before me."

Every morning Edmond was subjected to a
broadside of ribaldry such as we have described.
He was lucky if he escaped some form of punish-
ment. He would never have believed that his appearance could provoke such unfailing exacerba-
tion. There was no fatigue without him on it.
Latrine duty fell to his lot three times a week. He

hated the sergeant and the army with all his might.

One morning he reported sick. At the infirmary the doctor declared: "Sorry, I can do nothing for you. Try the vet."

Edmond, who really had a cold, was treated to a discourse on malingering and his tormentor did not overlook this chance to send him to the guard-room. He received another rebuff when he applied to join the cadet officers' squad. He was asked if he was crazy. "An officer with a dog's head!" they ex-claimed. "Whoever heard of such a thing! The men would mutiny. And what about army prestige? Have you thought of that?"

So he did not become an officer, as his education would have permitted; not even a corporal. He was overcome with despair and began to count the days to his discharge.

It is true to say that a regiment is a microcosm. Every type and every passion can be found in it. Edmond's dog's head drew out these passions and characters as litmus paper draws out acid. When-ever, from good or bad motives, the men gave him a thought, their feelings immediately assumed a sharpened and final shape. For example, there was in the company a skinflint who was always highly upset when he had to share his parcels among his comrades. On one occasion Edmond caught him devouring sardines all alone in the barrack-room.

"Give me one," he said. "I'm hungry."

The niggard, who never dared resist so direct a request for fear of reprisals, replied: "What, give my fine sardines to a guy with a dog's head? The hell with that!"

"My head allays his conscience," thought Edmond. "It legalizes his avarice. It reveals him to himself. What a treasure this head of mine is . . . for others!"

It happened that a re-enlisted quartermaster-sergeant with Socratic tastes made advances to him. "I like you a lot," he said. "You're a fine fellow. Nice-lookin', and your puppy-face tickles me. I've always had a weakness for doggies. Not to the point of going with them exactly, like in the *Bat d'Af.** But with you it's different. Say you like me a bit, Edmond! Want to make me happy? Y'know, you remind me of a drummer boy I knew, and your little mug, 's like Bonzo's—it gives me funny ideas."

Edmond rejected these proposals with horror,

* The Bataillon d'Afrique, a disciplinary corps in which conditions are extremely hard and vices are extremely developed.

but glimpsed fear in the eyes and uncertainty in
the voice of the quartermaster-sergeant. The latter
passed justifiably for a terrible fellow who knew
how to make the soldiers he fancied submit to his
desires; but in the present case bestiality was added
to sodomy and he hesitated to go as far as that.

Edmond was overcome with sadness at the sight
of these excesses. At night, lying on his palliasse in
the guardroom, he told himself bitterly: "I am
alone. There's no one like me. Not a soul. The
proof of it is that men have to bare their very souls
before they can reach me."

The top sergeant kept a petulant eye on the
growth of Edmond's fur and pitilessly made him
visit the barber twice a month. He also compelled
him to shave his whiskers and chops every day, so
that the unfortunate fellow's head was perpetually
inflamed and aching. His black snout, standing out
against his pink, sore skin, aroused great excitement among the soldiers. They played pranks on
him. One morning he woke to find his ears knotted
in a bun. They took advantage of his sleep to slip a
muzzle over him, which he had a dreadful time
getting off and which prevented him from drinking
his coffee. They surreptitiously tied a saucepan to

his tunic. Once he had to go down to parade in a false beard which he hadn't been able to remove. The usual regimental jokes acquired a special flavor when he was their victim. His dog's head, when he discovered some new practical joke against him, wore an expression of such distress, such helplessness and such bewilderment that his companions were unfailingly convulsed with laughter. At heart Edmond was by no means helpless or distressed. He did not care a rap if they put dung in his shoes or smeared boot polish over a sensitive part of his body; a bit of cleaning and it would vanish. But he could not control the expression in his eyes, or of his jaws and snout, which merely reflected an obscure and terrified awareness of what was happening. The stupidest Breton or the most dim-witted *chtimi* * could not offer anything like so enjoyable a spectacle.

One must not conclude from this rather somber picture that barrack life was all misery for Edmond. It must be remembered that these adventures have been reported in succession, crammed into a few pages. They were in fact spread over a whole year.

* Slang word used to describe a man from northern France.

Edmond had long periods of tranquillity and, indeed, was hardly more unhappy than any other soldier. Occasionally he joined forces with his comrades to rag the new recruits. As he was witty and good at telling spicy stories, he had a ready audience. Gradually he acquired a few reasonably loyal friends, who rarely turned against him. The company nicknamed him "Duduche," which he retained to the end of his service. They usually said: "Duduche has an ugly mug but he's a good chap."

In the end the very harshness of the top sergeant turned in Edmond's favor. The men felt he did not deserve such treatment. Soldiers who provoke the vindictiveness of their superiors enjoy the consideration of their equals. They were sorry for Edmond and let him share in their carousals. He learned how to get drunk on *vin rouge*.

One night, after libations at the Rendezvous des Industriels et des Commerçants, an obscure pub in Brioude, he laid a bet that he would steal a chicken. Lurching and singing down the dark streets, he made his way toward a henhouse he had located. Suddenly, yielding to a drunken whim, he began to bark. This both amused him and incited him to further efforts. He barked in a remarkable way. It became a sort of canine song, ranging from shrill to raucous, made up of roulades, howls of misery, yells of rage, yappings of joy and amorous supplications. His voice expressed the whole range of canine passions. Never had he felt so happy. He barked a veritable spaniel's Magnificat. He invented unheard-of modulations. He chanted a psalm of joy, fidelity and suffering. He intoned the fox hound's song of triumph, the bulldog's hymn, the poodle's canticle. This stirred up all the dogs in the town. In five minutes they struck up a concert. Watch dogs wrenched at their chains with a baleful rattling; dogs in flats leaped about frantically. They all vied with one another in giving tongue. This merely stimulated Edmond. He drew exquisite inspiration from these innumerable echoes. Brioude resounded with barking. One after another, windows were lit, but the inhabitants could find no reason for the din. Men could be seen, out chasing their dogs. Bitches in heat, taking advantage of the uproar, put their unhoped-for liberty to shameless profit. Cats, with their hair standing on end, ran spitting through the shadows. Edmond staggered no longer: he advanced with majesty. A bibulous voice within him murmured: "I am king of the dogs. They assemble at the sound of my voice. They will make me ruler of the world!" He entered the henhouse, seized a panic-stricken fowl in his jaws, and clenched his teeth till he felt the hot blood on his chops. At the Rendezvous his cronies asked him: "What's happened to you? You look like a dope."

For sole reply, Edmond threw down before them the hen, which he had still had in his mouth, then collapsed and vomited for several minutes. An hour later he climbed the barrack wall, crept into the dormitory and fell into a leaden sleep. The next morning, on parade, he looked so menacing that the top sergeant hoped he would attack him. It would be a chance to have him court-martialed. Edmond never budged and the poor man was disappointed.

It was in the army that Edmond first made acquaintance with love. He went with his comrades to the Brioude brothel. Strange *début*: the prostitute on whom his choice alighted began by uttering piercing screams.

"Who do they take me for?" she shrieked. "I'm

ready to go to bed with any man, but not with a dog. I'm not an animal!"

Edmond was agonized. Scenes of this nature can provoke nervous disorders. Why, it was only his head that was doglike! The rest of his person was human. If the head represents only one-seventh of the body, as they teach at art schools, then he was six-sevenths man and only one-seventh dog. True, it is chiefly the head that one sees; the rest is hidden under clothing. Nobody could guess that Edmond possessed the handsome, triangular torso and slender limbs of an ancient Egyptian and that these were all perfectly smooth-skinned. His comrades, it must be admitted, showed some discomfort, but, after a moment's hesitation, they took his side. They argued with the prostitute, affirmed that, apart from his head, Edmond was as manly as could be, declared that he had the best character in the world, etc. They emphasized his generosity, and this final argument won her over. Edmond, petrified, uttered not one word.

"Give her fifty francs," whispered a friend.

Edmond thrust a note into the prostitute's hand. She was not an unkind woman, and her profession had taught her not to play the prude for too long.

"All I ask of you," she said, "is not to kiss me. You haven't got fleas, I hope? D'you swear you are made like a man?"

When they came down again, the trollop had lost many of her prejudices against Edmond. She even ogled him quite tenderly.

"He was a virgin," she confided to her colleagues. "He doesn't look it, but he's ever so nice. And then, that dog's tongue of his is a scream!"

The brothel at Brioude is the saddest thing in the world. There is one square parlor, its walls covered with large mirrors. This is lit by a multitude of red and green lights, strung along below the cornice. Five or six not very desirable women constitute the establishment's livestock. Garbed, in winter and summer alike, in bathing dresses of faded colors and high-heeled, patent-leather shoes, they circulate between the tables, take up poses on the imitation-leather benches and betray a sad lack of imagination in their advances. The extreme wretchedness of this spectacle afflicted Edmond, whose one impulse was to escape. He rose to go. The prostitute shouted to him: "Bye-bye then, big dog. Must come again, eh?"

He never went back and kept a bitter memory of that evening. In his hard bed he thought things over. The emotional solitude into which his dog's head thrust him had inclined him toward soliloquy. "So now I know all about love," he told himself. "Love consists of going to the brothel at Brioude, pulling a bathing dress off a rather battered creature of thirty-five, and fornicating. Am I right or wrong to feel so blue? Wrong, no doubt. Anyway, now I've lost my virginity. That's a great advantage, though I wonder if it is really good for my character to have lost it in that way. Pray to heaven that the old girl's horrified screams don't haunt me all my life. I'd risk becoming impotent forever or hopelessly timid. It's true that in the end I emerged with honor and was found worthy of interest. But no, the spell is broken: I won't incur any fiascos. I've no reason to be sorry for myself." Had he been less innocent, Edmond would have drawn still more encouraging conclusions; had he been less young, he would have taken the matter more to heart. However, his escapade had left him with a strong feeling of uneasiness. With this he fell asleep, despite his deliberations.

It is curious to note that the only thing which

Edmond really liked about the regiment was the parades, the soldier's usual nightmare. As for him, he would have been very well suited with a parade and march-in-review every day. To march in the middle of the ranks, with five men on his left, four on his right, nine in front and ten behind, filled him with a real, sensual pleasure. His dog's head was reduced to an insignificant particle submerged amidst two hundred identical soldiers. It ceased to exist, so to speak. The band played a rousing tune; Edmond advanced with measured tread. The swing of the platoon carried him away. Humanity absorbed him. He felt a man among men, a French-man among Frenchmen.

What a grand day it was, nevertheless, when he could cry, *"Vive la classe!"* It marked the end of a year of mortal boredom. He duly took his military equipment to the stores and drew his receipt. The top sergeant benignly said to him: "We shall miss you, Du Chaillu. Why don't you sign on again?"

Edmond burst out laughing. "Re-enlist! That takes the cake! As regimental mascot, perhaps?"

"You are wrong, Du Chaillu," replied the top sergeant. "Stay in the army. You'll find your head less trouble there than anywhere else."

THREE

E DMOND'S year of military service proved fatal to his parents' affection for him. In truth, a year's absence was enough for them to forget their son and realize how pleasant it was not to have an offspring with a dog's head. M. and Mme Du Chaillu never made this horrible admission to each other, but they could not overlook the lightness in their hearts, their new taste for living, and their increasing good humor. They were both over sixty: suddenly they both felt twenty years younger. For twenty years they had not lived; the thought of their son, with his dog's head, had put every other preoccupation into the background. With this head removed from sight, they became themselves once more. Mme Du Chaillu bought herself a frivolous dress—white, with pink and blue flowers. This was hardly suited to a woman of sixty-two, but this woman of sixty-two had recaptured the soul of a young bride. M. Du Chaillu expressed delight in the dress. To follow suit, he trimmed his mustache and exchanged his pince-nez for tortoiseshell spectacles. One day he even made a bad pun. Mme Du Chaillu, who had not heard such excellent jokes as "Isabel necessary?" or "Ammonia a bird in a gilded cage" since Edmond's birth, shed several tears of joy. Finally, the old couple decided to go and spend a fortnight at Plombières, where they provide lightning cures for constipation.

Edmond naïvely expected a warm welcome from his parents. He had not informed them of the date of his discharge, intending to keep his return as a surprise. So one morning he rang the doorbell of the apartment in which he had passed his youth. His father's coldness and his mother's embarrassment nonplused him. He could not account, either, for the latter's being no longer dressed in black, or for the former's tortoiseshell spectacles.

After a few civilities and reciprocal information on states of health, M. Du Chaillu said: "Look, Edmond, here are six thousand-franc notes. They will help you along until you have found a job. I advise you to take a room in a small hotel with moderate rates. Young people must be given freedom. You wouldn't feel at ease here. Besides, we all know about youth: women, and all that sort of thing, my boy! And, anyway, we've taken over your room—your mother's made it her boudoir."

Edmond stuffed the notes into his pocket, kissed his papa and mama and went away, never to return. Since M. and Mme Du Chaillu, for their part, never gave any further sign of life, this was the last time he saw his parents. Such is the way in which one finally parts from those one loves best, without one word of explanation, without a gesture. Turning his father's last words over in his mind, Edmond came to the following conclusion: "My poor parents have grown away from me. These good people didn't deserve to have such a son. The remarkable thing is that they did not go crazy at my birth or present me to a menagerie. All the same, Papa might have gone a better way about kicking me out. And what about that precious job

47

he was to find me? I don't at all like his allusion to women. Considering my head, it was in bad taste."

Edmond took a room in the Hôtel de la Garonne, rue de Sommerard. Next, judging that liberty must also have some good points, he determined to buy a dog.

The Hôtel de la Garonne, rue de Sommerard, is frequented by students and artists, eccentric creatures, as we know. Its proprietor had, during forty years, witnessed so many practical jokes, seen his tenants so weirdly garbed, particularly at the time of the Bal des Quat'zarts, and harbored such exotic characters, that he had learned to be astonished at nothing. However, when Edmond had filled in the register, he looked at our hero over his glasses and said: "Are you French? Fancy that! I would never have believed it."

"Why?" asked Edmond.

"Oh, I don't know. You haven't the head of a Frenchman."

Edmond found this remark amusing and wanted to pursue the conversation. "What sort of head do you think I have?"

"Mustn't take offense," said the *patron*. "I didn't mean it seriously. I'm not like some people who hate all foreigners. Foreigners are just the same as us. French, Poles, Iroquois, they're all brothers, that's what I say."

"What did you think I was? A Kanaka or a Zulu?"

"Oh, I didn't think anything special. I said to myself: 'That gentleman must come from a hot climate. Africa or Tibet. Or perhaps a cold climate, since he's so shaggy.' In fact, I wasn't sure exactly. But since you're a Frenchman, let's take it that I said nothing."

"I have a dog's head," said Edmond coldly.

"A dog's head," protested the *patron*. "Come, come, we mustn't exaggerate."

"I know precisely how I stand."

"Well," said the *patron*, "so you have a dog's head. That's settled, then. Does that prevent your being French? Does that make you less intelligent than another? You have a dog's head. So what? My best clients were some Chinese. Well? Come, you mustn't worry, things will work out. You can have No. 17 on the second floor. There's a beautiful cupboard with a mirror, where you can hang your things."

In his bed, which creaked fearfully every time

49

he turned over, Edmond dreamed of the dog he would buy. "At last," he mused, "I am going to possess a good friend who, far from judging me or despising me, will consider me as a god. I'll feed him well and I'll never beat him. I will read vague and kindly thoughts in his eyes. We'll understand each other. I am sure that there are things in a dog's heart that no man has suspected and which I, surely, shall know how to decipher. . . . A dog! . . . I'm going to buy myself a dog! . . . My dream!" Edmond slept very badly, but his insomnia caused him no dismay. It was a wonderful insomnia.

The next morning, on entering the kennels, he trembled. A veritable anguish gripped him. "Come now," he reasoned with himself, "I'm only going to buy a dog, after all. What do they mean, these absurd physiological symptoms?" An exquisite sense of guilt, such as civilized occidentals doubtless experienced when confronted with the slave markets of Cairo in 1880, insidiously took possession of him. The strong canine odors of the place disgusted him, but the spectacle of twelve or fifteen dogs locked up in small cages, awaiting a purchaser, fascinated him. A young Belgian cattle-dog, elemental as a peasant, slim, agile and alert, soon claimed his attention. There was something both gentle and brutal about this animal which captivated Edmond. The dog eyed him insolently. A beautiful pink tongue lolled out of its half-open mouth. Edmond could not resist it. The kennel-mistress, after considering him, said: "If I were in your place, sir, I wouldn't buy a dog at all, and this one less than any other."

"But I am absolutely determined to buy a dog," said Edmond. "I've wanted one for a long time."

"Think it over carefully. You have lived without a dog until now. Go on doing so. It's much better, sir, believe me."

"What an odd woman," thought Edmond, but the lady's words impressed him.

"And why shouldn't I buy a dog?"

"I really can't explain," said the woman. "It's simply a feeling I had when I saw you. With your physique, you know . . ."

"Nothing will stop me buying a dog."

"Then take a cocker, or a poodle—a gentle dog that's easy to live with. What would you say to a dachshund? They are witty, quick-tempered and engaging. Just exactly what you want."

"No," said Edmond. "I want that Belgian cattle-dog."

"Be careful. He will make you unhappy. He's an uncontrollable, violent and impulsive creature with an unpredictable temper, who loves and hates without restraint."

"It is just for that that I like him," said Edmond.

"Oh, yes," resumed the woman in a pensive tone. "It is probably written in heaven that, if you are to have a dog, it is to be one like him. Have you made up your mind? Will you take him?"

"With my eyes shut," cried Edmond.

Shy as a bridegroom, he received the leash from the owner's hands, summoned a taxi and returned straight to the Hôtel de la Garonne. On seeing the dog, the proprietor playfully cried out: "Is that your little brother you're bringing in, M'sieu Edmond?"

"My big brother," replied Edmond, who was beside himself with joy.

The dog was perfectly beautiful. His head was not made ridiculous by a man's body. Edmond christened him "Henri," hoping by this human name to convey to the dog a sort of ambiguity which would bring him closer in spirit. An intellectual's daydream! Henri was an ordinary dog, moved by obscure atavisms. His ancestors had herded cattle since time immemorial. He himself was not very demonstrative. He was a rough, thick-set animal with a piercing eye and a shaggy coat. Edmond never wearied of admiring his proportions, his strength and his air of rigid nobility. He thought that Charlemagne's barons must have had a similar bearing. A vague feeling of inferiority came over him: the spaniel is less distinguished than the Belgian cattle-dog.

Edmond disconcerted Henri. The first day, Henri seemed to accord to his master the due respect of a quadruped for a vertical being, but that same evening a most painful scene occurred: Edmond, in wishing Henri good night, conceived the idea of rubbing his head against the dog's. How can one tell what goes on in the murky brains of a Belgian cattle-dog? Henri growled and bit Edmond viciously in the ear. The latter, bleeding, raised his arm. Henri crouched for battle, but Edmond's arm remained suspended. "Who am I," murmured our hero, "to assume the right to strike a dog?" He bathed his wound and went most unhappily to bed. This beginning augured ill for the future, but his passionate nature prevented him from adopting the necessary attitude. He stroked Henri with fervor, let him eat from his plate and sleep on his bed. Sometimes he took his head between his hands and looked deep into Henri's eyes. Alas, in that gaze he could read nothing but boredom or hostility. He never unleashed him in the street for fear that a car might run over him. He was proud, too, that passers-by should realize he was the owner of such a beautiful creature. Henri found Edmond's love hard to endure. A dog knows well how to show that he is being pestered. Henri growled when his master leaned over him. He never wagged his stump of a tail in Edmond's presence. If Edmond promised himself the pleasure of an evening's *tête-à-tête* with Henri in his room, the latter stretched out in a corner and slept. Whenever Edmond timidly went to stroke him, he woke with a bound and made as if to bite him. On the other hand, Henri was very fond of the proprietor of the Hôtel de la Garonne, who gave him bones and dug him heartily in the ribs. It was torture for Edmond to see his dog, so downcast when in his presence, become high-spirited and playful whenever his landlord appeared. He began to develop a feeling of hatred for the man, and had almost decided to move out when Henri ran away. They had lived together for a fortnight. Edmond ran in despair to the Lost Dogs' Home, hunted high and low and put up notices promising a reward, but all in vain. He regretted not having listened to the kennel-mistress. His landlord summed up this wretched experience: "Let me tell you, M'sieu Edmond, sentiment will never get you anywhere. You don't know how to go about it. You loved your dog too much, and it got on his nerves."

At these words, spoken in a tone of sincere friendship, Edmond's hatred subsided. They also caused him to reflect. "It is true," he told himself, "that my head makes sentimentality dangerous where I'm concerned. I am neither man nor dog. My nature pleases nobody. Tact, dexterity and guile, that's what I must use if I want to be loved." Unfortunately, Edmond was incapable of guile. His dual quality embarrassed him too much for him ever to play a part with success. Pursuing his meditations, he came to the conclusion that he must choose between dog and man. "I choose man," he swore solemnly to himself. "It is a question of rise or decline. My father was right. Dog is Darkness; Man is Light."

The world of men was not so easily stormed. Ed-

mond found this out when he set himself seriously
to find a job. His father's bank notes were drawing
to an end and it was becoming imperative to earn
some more. Naturally, Edmond turned first to the
more liberal professions and tried to exploit his
degrees. A solicitor who needed a clerk refused
him admittance to his office.

"I am the head of an important firm," the solicitor explained. "I'm sure you are a deserving young
man; your appearance, however, would contribute
too freakish a touch."

In truth, Edmond's head, standing out against
a background of files, had a playful aspect which
conformed ill with the austerity of the place.

A lawyer who needed a secretary held forth to
him as follows: "Awfully sorry, old boy, but can
you see yourself pleading petty cases in place of
me? Look at yourself, my friend! Your ears would
flap as much as your sleeves. You'd be the laughing-
stock of the Bar, and so would I for employing you.
Can you frankly see yourself in a lawyer's rig?"

No, Edmond had to admit he could not see himself in these garments. He thought for a moment
of presenting himself at the examination for the
Bench, but he pictured himself clothed in ermine

and wig, as president of the chamber. That stopped him short. There was nothing to be done with his law degree. Perhaps his degree in arts would prove more useful. He applied to the University for an interim post as master at a provincial school. The inspector-general summoned him and sadly imparted to him: "You are merely a graduate. You realize, naturally, that your—how shall I put it?—hmm . . . physiognomy places an additional (albeit slight) obstacle before the good will of the Alma Mater. Clearly, if you were a qualified teacher, it would be a different matter. But you are not a qualified teacher, and there's the rub."

"Sir," said Edmond, "you are a hypocrite. You refuse me a deputy post because I have a dog's head, and not because I am not a qualified teacher."

"Exactly, sir, since you oblige me to speak the truth. We have judged it inopportune to impose a master with a dog's head on our pupils, above all, a classics master. The pursuit of their studies and the development of their characters might be unpleasantly disturbed by it."

Edmond was brave. These unfruitful attempts did not discourage him. The Ministry of the Interior was enrolling draftsmen. He passed the exam brilliantly but was pitilessly turned down at the private interview. Meanwhile, in order to subsist, he gave Latin lessons for which he was paid half fees because of his head. Despairing of his diplomas, he fell back on less exalted occupations: hospital attendant, grocer's assistant, unskilled laborer. At the hospital he was told that he would give the patients nervous shocks; at the factory that his presence would start a strike; at the grocer's that he would chase away clients. They would only take him on as a night watchman. It was Edmond who refused this. "I'd rather die of hunger," he said, "than act as a watchdog."

Night watchman! The idea of it pierced his heart. So this was all that was offered him, all that he was considered fit for, he, Edmond, who had chosen to be a man! He brooded over this humiliation the whole day long. That night, alone in his room in the Hôtel de la Garonne, his grievances rose up in a lump in his throat: his wordless rupture with his parents, his disastrous adventure with Henri, the rebuffs which he had just endured. He spent three hours in front of his wardrobe mirror. On his bedside table there was a bowl of water in which he had dissolved ten tablets of veronal. He scrutinized himself in the glass. Never had he studied himself as earnestly as that night. He had a full-length reproduction of himself before his eyes. A dark-blue dressing gown enveloped him, leaving visible a triangle of his man's chest and his animal's neck. He was wearing rather narrow black trousers and small, polished pumps. He examined his dog's head with despair. He observed his flat, slightly concave skull, covered with a multitude of fine, gleaming hairs, arranged in yellow and white streaks; his dangling, furry ears, pink inside, which he had so often tried to pass off as artistic locks; his long muzzle, with the dry and wrinkled nose of a sick dog. "Night watchman! Night watchman!" he repeated in a frenzy. "It is to this that men reduce me! To the role of a dog. And dogs do not even respect the man in me. I'm a pariah, an untouchable, plague-stricken, an equivocal character from whom everyone turns aside. No, try as they like, they won't reduce me to a mere cur. I'll be a man or I'll kill myself." He curled back his lips, inspected his fangs, drew in his flat and nimble tongue, closed his eyes and opened them again. In short, he wanted to find something *attractive* about himself: he searched his face (what a word, applied to him!) for something human. "A sign, just one little sign of humanity—not even a sign, a mere glimmer," he told himself eagerly, "and I am saved! One glimmer and I'll pour the veronal down the lavatory! One fleeting spark is enough to live for, enough to give me tons of hope." His very eyes, moist and golden, on which he had so often been complimented, were completely canine. They expressed what the eyes of every spaniel in the world express: a canine goodness, naïveté and affection. Despair and a desire for self-destruction welled up in Edmond's human chest. He was about to break down in his loneliness and grief when suddenly the spark appeared in his eyes. Shaking with sobs, his mouth twisted in pain, he cried: "My despair is not a dog's despair!"

He collapsed onto his bed and wept for a long time like a dog, that is to say, without tears, but uttering low whines. It is one of the great advantages of Man that tears bring much speedier relief than that low whining. When he finally recovered his calm, Edmond got up, returned to the mirror and bared his side teeth, which was his way of smiling. He considered his head with friendly feelings. He had to take a second look to be completely consoled. Suddenly he fell madly in love with this spaniel's head. It belonged to him. It was his head, full of his thoughts, conscious of him, the controller of his acts, the source of his sorrows, an additional reason for living. He must raise himself to the peak of his amazing destiny, be proud of it and make it a source of pride, in the same way as an artist's vocation, a great singularity gives meaning to life.

Still illuminated by this memorable evening, Edmond found himself the next day being offered a place in a bank. This time he accepted; to be a bank clerk is not degrading. We will pass over the stupefaction of his colleagues and the clients of the bank when he took possession of his pay-counter. Both soon became used to him. The cashier alone, a surly old devil obsessed with conventionality, found his presence hard to stomach. He regarded it as a sign of the confusion of our age. He had had his baptism of fire at the Crédit Lyonnais before the 1914 war, when employees were obliged to wear a frock coat and a mustache.

"Everything's going to rack and ruin," he said. "One day someone comes to the office in a sport jacket, and the next we take on a clerk with a dog's head. What the bank will be like in ten years' time I dread to think. Anyway, it's all one to me; I shall have retired."

The other employees were not afraid of Edmond: with such a head he would not climb very high in the banking hierarchy. As for the clients, they were not slow to appreciate his prompt service and good breeding. Edmond was, furthermore, a curiosity which drew attention to the establishment. With his butterfly collar, his bow tie and his lutestring sleeves, he made a rather picturesque figure, we must admit. The manager of the bank delivered a short speech of welcome: "I think, M. Du Chaillu, that you appreciate to its full extent the spirit of understanding and tolerance which we have displayed in offering you a post. I have the pleasure to inform you that, so far as I am concerned, you have made an excellent impression. I think I'm a good judge of faces, and yours inspires my confidence. You have an unmistakably honest and studious appearance. I hope you will see to it that you don't disappoint us."

Apart from the friendly talk of the proprietor of the Hôtel de la Garonne, these were the first kind words that Edmond had heard for a long time. The manager had the kind, fat face of a superior wage-earner, capable of thinking on occasion of something other than his work. When he held out his hand to Edmond to show that the interview was over, the latter, instead of shaking it, raised it to his mouth and swept it with a great lick; then, horror-struck, he fled, cursing this ridiculous impulse. The manager, somewhat flabbergasted, wiped his hand, turned to his desk and muttered: "Poor fellow! He's not used to being shown any kindness."

Edmond, behind his grill, reviled himself: "What on earth possessed me? I've terrified the poor man. He's bound to sack me. Fancy licking people's hands just because they are nice to you! My word, I must be going mad! Good Lord, but that's a dog's reaction! How dreadful! I must keep an eye on myself." Sick at heart, he waited for the manager to appear. At the end of two hours, he went and knocked on his door. "I want to beg your pardon, sir . . ." he stammered. "For just now . . . you know . . . I can't think what came over me . . . I apologize for such an absurd gesture. It was utterly uncalled for."

"That's all right," said the manager. "We'll forget it. You're too emotional. But it's quite excusable; your action was prompted by a good heart."

The tribulations of a bank employee with a dog's head. There's a fine subject, a mine of possibilities, of comic or explosive details. Alas, there is nothing to tell in this instance. Edmond was a model clerk, full of good will and resourcefulness. It was impossible to find fault with his work; he performed it meticulously. It never occurred to any client to pass his hand through the grill and scratch his occiput. Nobody wiped a pen on his ears. Nobody told him he ought to have been set to guard the strongroom. His only misadventures were concerned with love, and that the bank should have formed their setting was a mere coincidence.

A few feet away from Edmond a young girl attended to shares and securities. Her name was Marianne: she was twenty and her father was a police constable. Her Parisian little face—small nose, small eyes and small white teeth; her charming figure; her pretty, teasing ways; all made Edmond fall in love with her. It was madness. Marianne had a vulgar little soul, and vulgar souls are not likely to fall for our hero.

Edmond was jubilant. A woman inspired in him

the most human of all feelings. "I am in love like a man," he reflected. "There's no mistake about it. Marianne is a young girl and I desire her. What luck! And how pleasant it is to love!"

He was so carried away that he did not even aspire to be loved in return. Marianne, however, was not indifferent. Thus, at the bank, she was the first to show interest in him. For three or four days she showered her smiles upon him. She was a flirt. She was not above seducing Edmond. He was sufficiently emboldened to respond with affectionate waves of the hand. Once, when he was sweating over a statement of accounts, Marianne approached him softly and, without his noticing, adorned his head with a pink ribbon. Such familiarity enchanted Edmond. From her counter Marianne would make faces at him. He replied by wrinkling his muzzle or taking his ears between his teeth. In short, a relationship of childish, affectionate nonsense was established between them and it convinced Edmond that Marianne was the only person in the world who understood him.

Each morning on arrival she would whisper in his ear: "Who would like a lump of sugar?" Then she took a piece from her bag and laid it on Edmond's table. The latter had a sweet tooth—a canine trait—and this daily token of attention thrilled him. A month later Marianne ventured now and then to stroke Edmond's muzzle. These contacts stirred him deeply. When she placed her hand on his fur, he would close his eyes and sigh. How could he help feeling happy? A pretty girl loved him. Can one resist a pretty girl when one has a dog's head? Like his schoolmates, Marianne jokingly called him "Toby-dog" or "Bonzo," but it had quite a different ring. Almost tenderly she would inquire: "Well, how's my little Bonzo?"

Could he be angry when, at lunchtime, she asked: "At what restaurant is Bonzo going to gnaw his bone today?"

She would bring him stamps to lick; she would say: "My, what big teeth you have!" To which he fatuously replied: "All the better to bite you with, my girl!"

But Edmond's real happiness was to hear his beloved call him "Marianne's own little bowwow." Love is composed of such follies.

One evening Marianne accepted an invitation of Edmond's. As she was rather ashamed of appearing publicly in such company, she fixed a rendezvous

at a cinema. Edmond loved the cinema, where nobody can see you and you may forget yourself for
a couple of hours, but on this occasion he hardly
looked at the film—his neighbor disturbed him too
much. He took her hand. She let him hold it and
he, idiot that he was, passed a whole hour squeezing
it without daring to press further. Edmond sensed,
however, that there was something yielding about
Marianne. If at that moment he had dragged her
out of the cinema, put her in a taxi and taken her
to the Hôtel de la Garonne, he could have possessed
her. Marianne was a depraved little person. For
the length of two hours she was eaten up with
curiosity at the idea of making love with a man-dog.
Alas, Edmond failed to seize his opportunity. He
was inexperienced. Marianne felt suddenly overcome with shame. She whipped her hand away
from Edmond and said: "Let's go. I've had enough.
I want to go home."

In the street Edmond tried to put his arm round
her waist. She eluded him, fixed him with steely
eyes and spat out: "Heel, Fido! Down, sir!"

These words, spoken harshly and without her
customary pleasantness, seemed to Edmond exactly
what they were: outrageous. He saw Marianne

home in silence. At her door he raised to her the eyes of a heartbroken spaniel, while she abruptly threw her arms round his neck and gave him three kisses, one on the muzzle, one on the ear and one on the eye.

"*Au revoir*, Fido," she murmured. "No nights in the kennel for me."

"Ah, well," thought Edmond, as he trudged back to the Hôtel de la Garonne. "That's the end of the affair. I'll never sleep with Marianne now. And, what's more, it's my fault! A little more determination and . . . Well, better forget it. Draw a veil . . ."

Though sorry to have lost the Marianne he loved, he was conscious of a sort of melancholy happiness at finding himself once more alone in the world. "Lord, thou hast made me mighty and alone . . ." he declaimed beneath a lamppost in the rue Cukas.

"Is that you, M'sieu Edmond?" cried the proprietor when he entered the hotel. "Come in and chat for a minute if you're not too tired."

It was past midnight. The hotelkeeper was reading a novel below the keyboard, in his shirt sleeves.

"You're looking out of sorts," he exclaimed when he saw his lodger. "Another dirty trick been played on you? I'll get you a drop of brandy. That'll put you on your feet. Would you like a biscuit?"

"Thank you," said Edmond, accepting this refreshment.

"What's wrong?" resumed his landlord. "You look very down in the mouth. Another dog story, I'll bet. Take it from me, M'sieu Edmond, you shouldn't go with dogs. They'll only bring you mortification. You know, I once had a client who had unusual habits. He was a very well-educated gentleman, very nice and friendly. He used to bring back sailors or little boys that he picked up in Montmartre. Well, you've no idea how they made him suffer. They beat him up, they pinched his money, they insulted him. It made no difference; he just went back for more. I warned him more than once, I assure you. Advised him to be careful. Not a chance! One day he was so unhappy that he went and threw himself into the Seine. That's how these affairs end up, M'sieu Edmond. You shouldn't let yourself be dragged into them."

Edmond could see no connection between the landlord's story and his own case, but he hadn't the courage to explain the cause of his distress.

"What you need, M'sieu Edmond," continued

69

the other, "is to marry. That's my advice. Not a young girl—they only think of sleeping around and having a good time—but someone who's already had a bit of experience and knows what life is like. Apart from your head, you're quite a fine-looking fellow. And even your head isn't a bad one of its kind, whatever people may say. Me, I always say a man doesn't need good looks."

"There's the difference of heaven and hell between being ugly and having a dog's head," said Edmond.

"Oh come, M'sieu Edmond, you mustn't say that. You don't know women as I do."

By the time his landlord had poured out a fourth glass of brandy Edmond was transformed into a lighthearted, optimistic being who sincerely believed the adage: "For one lost there are ten found." All his past life seemed to him at this moment like some monstrous and ignoble stutter. How could he have fallen into so many errors, groped in the dark for so long? Thank heaven he now knew his true nature! The highest destiny awaited him. His spaniel's head? To think that he had looked on it as a disgrace! On the contrary, it was a formidable asset; what victories would he not win with this head from now on? Going up to bed, he chuckled and smugly repeated: "Alcohol isn't made for dogs."

The next morning Marianne didn't speak to Edmond. At noon, as he was pulling off his lute-string sleeves, she came up to him and, turning to their colleagues, who were tidying their papers or putting on their overcoats, she cried: "Come and watch a dog do his tricks."

She turned to Edmond. "Well, hasn't Bonzo had his lump of sugar today?"

Edmond was speechless with misery at seeing the girl he loved indulge in such disgraceful behavior. Marianne sniggered.

"Look!" she continued, taking a piece of sugar from her bag, "you can have it if you sit up and give me your paw."

She balanced the sugar on Edmond's muzzle, but he lowered his head and it fell off.

"Well," said Marianne, "for a dog who can talk you're not very sharp. Do you know how to 'die for your country'? No. Not even that. The truth is, you don't want to, you little cur. Ah, I've got it! He wants to jump. Someone bring a hoop for Fido, and he'll hop through it. What a joke, boys!"

It is always upsetting to be present at the sudden and complete betrayal of one on whose good faith one has relied. Marianne showed no further trace of friendship; she had become an implacable enemy. Edmond was not prepared for this. His colleagues, embarrassed, wanted neither to annoy Marianne by open censure nor to wound Edmond by exaggerated hilarity. Hence their ambiguous attitude, their ashamed smiles, their timid gestures of disapproval. The cashier, standing with his overcoat half on, watched the scene in dismay.

"This sort of thing wouldn't happen in a bank," he said, "if only they didn't engage little chits and dog-headed clerks."

Edmond feared two things: that the manager might come out of his office and that Marianne might describe the previous evening. The manager did not appear, but Marianne, altering her tone, said: "Ladies and gentlemen, did you know that Bonzo took me to the cinema last night?"

Despite himself, Edmond's ears flattened against his head, like a spaniel about to be whipped by his master.

"And then," continued Marianne, "d'you know what happened? He tried to kiss me. Exactly.

Bonzo's like that. It's his age. Don't you think it's time we found him a bitch? He might turn dangerous. Dogs are all alike, I'm told, in love with their mistresses. The trouble is that I don't like dogs. Let the mistress stick to her bed and the dog to his basket, that's what I always say. Aren't I right?"

Their colleagues didn't know where to look. In all his life Edmond had never seen such an embarrassed crowd. One of them, toward whom Marianne more directly turned to throw out her "Aren't I right?," thinking himself personally addressed, replied in a pitiful and cowardly voice: "Er . . . yes, in a sense . . . but we mustn't generalize."

At this, Edmond put on his hat and left. In the afternoon a young man at the paying-in desk came and gave him a friendly slap on the shoulder. "Mustn't take on too much, old chap. All women are harpies." This phrase comforted Edmond greatly.

Nevertheless, it had become most painful for him to meet Marianne. He handed in his notice.

"Good-by, Du Chaillu," said the manager. "I shall miss you as a sensible and diligent member of the staff. I hope you have been happy with us

and that no one, during your brief stay, has in-
dulged in any jokes in bad taste about you."

"Nobody, sir," replied Edmond. "Everyone has
been most kind to me. I shall have nothing but
happy memories of this firm."

It was all Edmond could do not to lick the manager's hand again. This good man inspired in him
an extraordinary tenderness. In his hotel bedroom
he exhorted himself: "No, it can't go on like this.
I've got to get out of this mess. I must sum and
weigh things up, make out my account. What
claims can I have? What shall I ever achieve? First,
take love: what woman have I the chance of sleeping with? Even with gentleness, fidelity and affection, I'll never succeed in seducing any normal
girl or woman. What's left, then? Prostitutes and
depraved creatures. I don't much like the idea, but
so much the worse for me. It's a line to take and
it's better than chastity. Second: money. I need a
lot. Semi-poverty with a dog's head is quite impossible. I must have a fine house, good clothes, a
car, etc. Money will obtain me as many women as
I like. I could travel. I could go to Egypt. Third,
politics: futile to think of them. The country would
never tolerate a President of the Council with a

spaniel's head. Ah, if it were only a bulldog's. Fourth, friendship: I'm not worried on that score. Kindhearted and intelligent people will always like me. The whole problem boils down to earning a lot of money very quickly."

His balance sheet was not really so distressing. Two things alone were forbidden him: politics, for which he didn't care, and sentimental love. Bah! What was that? Many men have spent their whole lives without ever having been loved or having dabbled in politics—the philosopher Kant, and the painter Fra Angelico, to mention great men alone.

FOUR

E DMOND'S sojourn at the bank, albeit brief, had initiated him into the mysteries of finance. He decided to play the Stock Exchange. Now nothing is easier than playing the Stock Exchange: all that is needed is to buy low and sell high—a simple truth which no broker or speculator has ever understood. Edmond stuck to it rigorously and in a few months had made quite a fortune. These "few months" are of no interest to the student of psychology: during this time Edmond experienced no feeling at all except, perhaps, that of cupidity, and even this is uncertain. He thought of nothing but "Royal Dutch," "General Motors," "British Thomson-Houston," "Shanghai Tramways," "Anglo-Iranian Oil," "Rio Tinto," "United Shipping," and "East Rand." His head was filled with nothing but calculations, cold speculations, combinations. He read the financial journals, pensively sucking his ear. At first this unusual dabbler in stocks and shares was mocked, but speculators have little sense of humor: after Edmond had brought off some pretty transactions, he was promoted to a businessman, and this, in any case, is no subject for laughter.

When he left the Hôtel de la Garonne the proprietor bade him farewell. "You're a capitalist now, M'sieu Edmond. You've got plenty of gray matter, if you'll excuse my saying so. What I mean is, one mustn't go by appearances. To look at you, one would never think you were capable of accumulating a fortune."

"Where there's a will . . . ," said Edmond modestly.

"Beg pardon, but with a head like yours you need enough will for two. A face like that doesn't make things easy."

"You needn't tell me *that!*"

"Ah, but the world's a cruel place. After all, it isn't your fault if you're made that way."

"You are very kind," said Edmond, "but everything happens exactly as if it *were* my fault, and I sometimes wonder if I am really not responsible for my muzzle, snout, ears and fur. After all, one can't always be right in face of the whole world. The whole world seems to think it is I who have made myself such as I am. There must be some truth behind this idea."

"Your dog's head, M'sieu Edmond, has its good points. Would it ever have occurred to you to play the Stock Exchange without it? With a head like anyone else's, you'd have remained a black-coated worker all your life."

"Perhaps."

"You see? You're not to be pitied as much as all that. There are many men more unhappy than you. Tell me, what do you plan to do with your money?"

"What one usually does with money—spend it."

"You won't go buying any dogs?"

Edmond blushed.

"Don't buy any more dogs, M'sieu Edmond," repeated the landlord. "Take a friend's advice."

79

"Er . . . I don't know . . . ," mumbled Edmond.

"I'm fond of you, M'sieu Edmond. What I'm telling you is for your own good. Life's hard enough without actually looking for opportunities to make oneself unhappy."

"Well . . . good-by," said Edmond rather stiffly. "I shall retain pleasant memories of the Hôtel de la Garonne."

"Come and look us up sometimes," said the proprietor, who identified himself with the establishment and, like monarchs, referred to himself in the first person plural. "It will always be a pleasure to see you. I haven't often had tenants like you, let me tell you."

"That doesn't surprise me," said Edmond.

Edmond left the Hôtel de la Garonne to live in a little house he had bought at Louveciennes, which he had filled with Empire furniture, overloaded with griffons, sphinxes, lions and swans in bronze. He could not resist buying some statuettes by the animal sculptor Barye, and a superb "Sheepdog Pursuing a Sheep" by Rosa Bonheur. There was nothing premeditated about this choice: he had seen these works at an antique dealer's and took them because they pleased him. Somewhat later on, a "Woman with Dog" by Matisse made its appearance in his drawing room; Edmond would have been astonished had he been told that he liked this painting more for its subject than for its style. With the house Edmond bought a car and three dozen silk shirts. His plans began to materialize.

What caused him the most wonder about his new estate was to have servants who called him "Sir" and treated him with respect. "How far I've come since the bank," he thought with pride. "Today I am well dressed, I keep a good table and, above all, I have a man and a woman to wait on me. I despotically govern two beings endowed with human faces; two beings who, theoretically, are of a race superior to mine. I say: 'Albert, go and fetch my cigars!' or 'Rose, cook me a stuffed partridge!' and they reply: 'Yes, sir; certainly, sir; does Monsieur Edmond need anything else?' You must admit it's rather extraordinary when you think of it." Rose and Albert despised "Monsieur" no more than servants despise their masters in general. In the pantry they called him "The Monkey," * which, considering our hero's head,

* The slightly contemptuous name which French servants give their employers.

81

sounded rather strange; perhaps they did not fully appreciate its humor. They were both about fifty, a critical age for domestics: their vices had reached full development and old age had not yet begun to moderate them. Edmond was touched when he thought of Rose's and Albert's devotion. The latter was full of attention, the former lovingly cooked special dishes for him. Neither of them ever approached him without a broad smile. Whenever Edmond gently reprimanded them, they admitted their fault without demur and assured him that in the future they would be more careful. They recouped themselves behind his back: Albert smoked his cigars and Rose filched the housekeeping money, not to mention petty pilferings which were attributed to the negligence of the laundry, wear and tear, etc.

Rose enjoyed nothing so much as discussing her employer with the caterers and gossips she met at the market.

"How's your dog getting on, Rosie?" she was unfailingly asked every morning.

"Nicely, thank you," the cook would reply. "I've stewed his bone and he's quite happy."

"I say, Rose, it must be pretty handy to have a

boss like that. He licks the plates, which saves you washing them."

"That's what *you* think! He's like all dogs, trouble and bother."

"Is it your job to take him out to the lamppost?"

"No! Whatever do you think? That's the butler's job, that is. Me, I'm just the cook."

"Better give me some bones," she would tell the butcher, to the delight of his shop. "My master's very partial to 'em."

Edmond also played a large part in their pantry dialogues.

"Times must be pretty hard," said Albert, "for us to have to work for a chap like that. I don't know how you feel, Rose, but I can't get used to his mug. Every night I feel like telling him to go to his basket. To think it's guys like *him* that has the money, and it's *us* that has to empty their chamber pots!"

"A man who has a dog's head," replied Rose, "I don't call a man. If you ask me, it's a dirty shame that human beings has to work theirselves to the bone for the likes of him. Good thing we don't do badly here."

At other times Albert teased Rose for what he

pretended was the fascination Edmond exercised over her and, in lurid detail, would describe the latter in the throes of fornication. Rose held her sides with laughter. Between two gasps, she would whoop: "Stop it, or I'll split!"

In a whimsical moment, Edmond decided to open an account at the bank where he had worked. One morning he drove up, dressed in a superbly tailored suit, a carnation in his buttonhole, and with large tortoiseshell spectacles on his muzzle. Like an American businessman, he was smoking a cigar. His car waited at the door. His former colleagues couldn't believe their eyes. Edmond read on their faces a mixture of baseness and envy which was like balm to his soul. The surly cashier alone maintained the same attitude: a dog's head was to him as shocking on a financier's shoulders as on those of a bank clerk. The manager did not come out of his office, which upset Edmond, for he believed that in this man he had a friend who would rejoice at his good fortune. As for Marianne, she seemed very commonplace in her cheap little frock. At first she pretended not to notice him, but he had some shares to deposit and it was her duty to hand him the receipt. She finally came up to him and said shyly: "Can I help you, sir?"

Wealth brought Edmond great enjoyment. First, it canceled out his head. If he had not known how he stood, if he had not from time to time passed a mirror, nothing in the world could have made him believe he had a yellow and white spaniel's head. Oh, the sublime effect of bank notes! Overnight that hideous or ridiculous object became just anybody's head. No prostitute feigned disgust now. In the hotels, the porters displayed the same obsequiousness toward him as toward the film stars and millionaire tourists. At the Albergo Hassler in Rome a lift-boy was dismissed on the spot for daring to murmur in Italian: "Dogs must use the service stairs." Edmond finally realized that ninety per cent of women are for sale, and did not abstain from acquiring those whom he desired. It cost him somewhat more than other men, it is true, but was it not precisely in order to be able to buy what other men get for nothing that he had set about amassing a fortune?

Edmond never recalled this period without pleasure. It was undoubtedly the happiest time of

his life. Louveciennes was a charming place. He
entertained there admirably. For a whole year it
became the fashion to dine with him. The *Revue
des Ambassades* printed his photograph: in a gray
bowler hat, on the racecourse at Longchamp, he
was offering his arm to the Marquise de Merteuil.
He possessed everything that wealth permits: a
library, a cellar, dressing gowns, pictures. He even
devised a hobby for himself—the Minotaur—and
collected images of this fabulous being. In truth,
a bull's head appears even more incongruous on
a man's body than a dog's; and the legend of
Pasiphaë's child fascinated Edmond. For himself,
he would have had no objection to being confined
in the depths of a labyrinth, or having seven Athe-
nian beauties and as many youths sacrificed to him
every ten years. He took a great interest in com-
posite creatures and read with rapture tales of
centaurs, sirens and fauns. His library was distinguished by a fine Aldine folio of Ovid's *Metamorphoses,* with engravings.

Edmond plunged into the *Metamorphoses* as
into a novel. He identified himself with the tragic
destinies which Ovid narrates, as another reader
might with Stendhal's heroes. The hideous

Polyphemus saying to Galatea: "Myself but lately I beheld in the reflection of the limpid water; and my figure pleased me as I saw it," set him a-sighing. He was roused to indignation by the massacre of the centaurs by the Lapithae. On the other hand, Ovid's frank acceptance of unnatural subjects delighted him. There is no vice in Ovid: he lays down the principle of the brotherhood of all matter. A mere thread separates human flesh not only from the animal but also from the vegetable, the mineral, water, earth, air, the stars, and this thread is constantly snapped. Concupiscence is manifested with extreme liberty; union is accomplished between all species. The young men lust after Narcissus as much as the maidens. Io, become a heifer, retains her beauty to the point of inspiring desire. To seduce Europa, Jupiter assumes the shape of a bull and stirs her still more deeply in this guise. Pygmalion caresses an ivory statue which he covets as a woman. Salmacis and Hermaphroditus are mingled and fused into a single being because of Salmacis's excessive love. Arethusa is transformed into a fountain to escape from Alpheus, but the river recognizes in these waters the one he loves: in order to unite with her, he casts off his human shape and resumes his liquid form. Tiresias twice changes sex and knows the twofold pleasures of the senses. By dint of accompanying these amorous beings, with their yearning after shapes and substances utterly different from their own, Edmond ended by asking himself why he, too, should not become the object of someone's love. He lost all feeling of his oddity and of the horror he could inspire in women.

He understood marvelously well the grief of men changed into beasts—inability to express themselves, regret for the irremediable, and a profound feeling of subjection, for animals are always slaves. Io watched by Argus's hundred eyes was Edmond judged by men; Edmond again, Actaeon changed into a stag, the former huntsman now the prey torn by his own hounds and grieving not to witness the kill; Edmond, yet again, Callisto changed into a she-bear, on the point of being slain by her son, who fails to recognize her. Nobody recognized Edmond.

These tales comforted him. They showed him that his case was not unique. The world had known dual beings like himself—or had at least envisaged the possibility of their existence. Edmond had a deep conviction that men and beasts are made of the same flesh, animated by the same spirit, capable of uniting with each other. The ancients, close as they were to the birth of the world, knew this truth; but in three thousand years it had grown dim. In those days a dog's head was not a fatal curse. Today men believe that an impassable wall separates them from animals. They have no concern for them except to subject them to idiotic experiments. In contrast to the Roman she-wolf, to Amalthaea the goat, the fish Oannes, and Apis the bull, Edmond evoked the miserable experiments of Pavlov, who dedicated his life to studying the effects that the ringing of bells produced on dogs. Finally there was Egypt—but we mustn't anticipate.

All the same, whatever comfort Edmond drew from ancient superstitions, his head continued to haunt him and became an increasingly heavy burden. He had heard talk of plastic surgery. After some tergiversation, he determined to consult a man who had won fame by his restoration of several old actresses. The surgeon, accustomed to the strangest faces, betrayed no surprise. He answered Edmond's anxious inquiries in the calmest of tones.

89

"I can cut down your ears, make some skin grafts, pull out your fangs and have them replaced by gold teeth."

"No, no," cried Edmond. "I want a man's face, a real man's face, with an aquiline nose, a mouth with well-shaped lips, a high forehead. I want a flat, man's face, covered with smooth white skin. That's what I want, Doctor."

"Impossible."

"Why impossible? Everything is possible these days. I was told you could work wonders."

"I can work on a human face because all the parts are there, but, good God! I can't invent a chin for you, for example."

"Make me a face without a chin. It would always be better than a spaniel's head."

"A face without chin, mouth, nose or forehead? Do you want me to break up your bones and reduce your skull to pulp? And your tongue! Have you thought about your tongue? Where would we put it? It's too long."

These were words of despair. There was nothing to be done. Edmond was condemned to his head.

"Ah, Doctor," he cried in a fit of anger, "when I think of all the misfortune my head has brought

me, I tell myself that I have been the victim of a
legal error, that it's impossible that things should
go on like this to the end, that one day they will
revise my sentence. An animal's head is nothing,
but a spaniel's . . . Was there ever anything so
grotesque as a spaniel's head? A spaniel's head
does not even inspire horror, merely laughter. Why
haven't I a tiger's head, even a jackal's? . . . Not
only have I a dog's head but, aggravating circum-
stance, the head of the most ridiculous dog to be
found."

"Would you really rather I didn't cut down your
ears?" asked the surgeon. "It wouldn't hurt and
you wouldn't look like a spaniel any more."

"No," said Edmond. "Since you cannot mold me
the face of a man, I'll stay as I am. Cut down my
ears! Ugh! I should feel as if something were being
amputated."

"You could have yourself dyed black. . . ."

"Indeed!" cried Edmond bitterly.

For a month he shut himself up in his room,
stretched out on his bed. Albert brought him his
meals on a tray. Edmond was so deep in meditation
that his cigarettes singed his fur and burned his
chops before he put them out. He thought of his

head. "Why have I no faith?" he asked himself. "I could retire to a monastery for the rest of my days. Life isn't worth the trouble of living. I have done what I wanted: I have earned money, I have tasted all the pleasures given to men, and now here I am even more unhappy than when I was poor."

Previously he had been ashamed of his head in front of others. Now he saw with horror that he was ashamed of it before himself. He loathed it, not because of the mockery and insults which it brought upon him, but for its own sake. He had seen enough of it. It gave him nausea. In a flash of intuition he had perceived that this head was an absurdity, and that it was in him, Edmond, that this irreducible absurdity was lodged. Such an idea is enough to leave one prostrate for a month.

"He must have worms," suggested Rose. "That's what's got into him."

"If he had worms," replied Albert, "he'd rub his bottom on the carpet. All dogs do that."

Edmond did not kill himself. He went to see a psychoanalyst. He naïvely believed that the man would discover and root out his torments like bad teeth. The psychoanalyst questioned him about his childhood and his love affairs. He demanded details. After three hours' conversation, he cleared his throat and solemnly announced: "Your case is simple. It is all because you have a dog's head. . . ."

Edmond snatched up his hat and left, slamming the door. His month of seclusion had made him irascible. In the street he bethought himself of the Belgian cattle-dog whose master he had been for a fortnight. "Dear Henri," he mused, "why did you leave me? You and I could have lived happily together. Ah, if only I had you beside me at this moment, how I should enjoy stroking your head! I set about you the wrong way. But now I'm no longer the same man. I have matured. I should have the right approach. And why shouldn't I buy a dog? There's no one to whom I must render account. Now that I think of it, the happiest two weeks in my life were those I spent with Henri, who didn't love me."

Edmond didn't buy one dog, but four: a Great Dane, an Irish setter, an Alsatian and a poodle. The four beasts strained at their leashes, and Edmond, as they dragged him along, compared himself to a Roman patrician in his quadriga. His distress and metaphysical torments had vanished. He was burst-

ing with contentment. "I did quite right to buy
four," he told himself. "With one, I should have
loved him like an only son. He'd have made me
suffer."

At Louveciennes the two servants deliberated on
the course to be adopted before this canine in-
vasion, and, as a precaution, demanded an increase
in wages which Edmond, in his joy at owning four
dogs, granted them at once.

The dogs, besides the purity of their breed, each
had an interesting character. The huge, taciturn
Great Dane had a slow and deliberate gait: he was
too well aware of his strength to use it inconsider-
ately. Young and impulsive, the setter spent his
time playing with the poodle. The latter was intelligent, affectionate and resourceful. Lastly came
the Alsatian, who, owing to his austere habits and
a flaunted indifference toward everything, allied
himself with the Great Dane. Edmond, faithful to
the principle which had formerly dictated to him
the name of Henri, called the Great Dane Alexander, the Alsatian William, the poodle André and
the setter Lucien; but he refrained from repeating
the errors which had alienated Henri. With his
four dogs he behaved like a paterfamilias—im-

partial, sharing out affection in equal proportions, favoring none and indulging in no excess of demonstrativeness. This restraint cost him dear, for he longed to fondle André, dreamed of a hearty friendship with Alexander, etc. "I want my dogs to love me," he decreed. "I must not frighten them by ridiculous effusions. Dogs are like children: an overpassionate expression of love embarrasses them." It is likely that Edmond was mistaken and that dogs are not so touchy, but this time he was anxious not to suffer, and one cannot reasonably laugh at the clumsy attempts of a being to safeguard his heart.

A very pleasant existence now began for Edmond. He could not explain to himself why the presence in his house of four dogs, who lived with their animal dignity, should make him so happy. Thank heaven they got on well together: never a quarrel, never a fight, except in play. The mighty strength of Alexander, the Great Dane, was applied to pacific activities. William gave vent to his somber passions only toward strangers. As for the two innocents, Lucien and André, there was no wickedness in their hearts. "My goodness," said Edmond, "if I'd only known that the mere possession of these four dear creatures would bring me peace of mind, I'd have bought them long ago." He did not go so far as to analyze the affection he bore his dogs. It resembled nothing he had so far experienced. Edmond knew how to follow the processes of thought. Nurtured on the humanities, he had widely practiced the axiom "Know thyself"; but when he questioned himself thereon, his heart, that familiar territory, became shadowy and unknown. Perhaps there were thoughts in his dog's head of which he had never been aware. One does not possess a spaniel's head with impunity. Edmond, where the mind was concerned, believed himself to be a complete man. He spoke the language of Rivarol; he had had a full education and taken his degree; he directed his thoughts according to the method of Descartes. His sexual desires inclined him naturally toward women. He had once and for all laid down the principle that he was canine only in appearance, and it was precisely out of this that his troubles arose. With a mind as ambiguous as his body, he would not have been unhappy at all. From time to time the idea that the duality of his nature was not confined to his physique crossed his mind, but he paid it no attention. When he bethought himself to explore this instinct which constantly urged him toward dogs, which caused him to desire their company and made him vaguely melancholy and restless in their absence, the perfect, analytical mechanism of French education began to function within him. He held logical arguments with himself which led him quite clearly to such trite conclusions as: "If I love dogs, it is because they have qualities which make them lovable." In brief, Edmond completely failed to recognize his problem.

Lucien, André, William and Alexander, though mere dogs, understood it much better. Within a week they saw right through their master. One week more enabled them to put an end to the rather distant and overbearing attitude he affected toward them. It seemed as if they were guided by a superior spirit. We shall never know which first gave them a notion of their power: Edmond's head or an intuition of his weakness. It all began with a windowpane that William broke. Edmond, constrained to beat him, approached him with a whip. The dog cringed. Edmond struck. William whined softly and ran to hide in a corner of the garden, from which nothing could dislodge him. Meanwhile Edmond reproached himself for his brutality. "What is a windowpane to me when I have more money than I know how to spend? I've treated my poor William like a slave; I was ready to beat him for a piece of glass. If only I didn't hurt him too much! What will he think of me? I'll never do it again. No, no . . . anything rather than rule by terror." He paid a visit to William, made up to him, kissed him. Under the dog's gaze he felt prostrate with guilt; it was a beautiful look, full of despair, pride and wounded love.

"William, William, forgive me," said Edmond. "It gave me no pleasure to beat you. I did it simply to teach you that you must not jump through windows . . . because you might cut yourself."

William half rose and turned away, thus expressing the profound disappointment Edmond caused him. Edmond was beside himself. He knelt down, clasped the dog in his arms and pressed his head against William's. Finally the latter agreed to forgive him, but made it clear that he was not entirely won over. After this everything happened as if he had passed the word on to his comrades. They nosed out their master's congenital weakness. They took every advantage of it. Blackmail must be an elementary and natural activity since even dogs are capable of exercising it. Edmond offered no resistance to the determined front of these four rascals. His inclination was to endure anything provided his dogs were happy, for their happiness was the condition of his own. At first he tried to scold them, to raise his voice against them, but the dogs drew back and repelled all advances, even when accompanied by gastronomic appeasement. The slightest sign of bad temper ended by throwing Edmond into unbelievable distress. He questioned himself, endlessly, trying to discover in what way he had failed to please; he would stoop to anything to recover grace. His torturers in turn relieved themselves on the Persian carpets, ate off the Sèvres china and sharpened their claws on the Louis XV chairs. This much distressed Albert, who respected beautiful things, but Edmond replaced them one by one. To his servant's protestations he replied: "Never mind, Albert. They're my children. I like to see them enjoying themselves."

"But," objected Albert, "don't you see, sir, that they're treating you like a fool? It's not good for them to be allowed to develop bad habits like that."

Edmond did not question his happiness. In three

weeks the dogs had become the masters in his house. That was all right. He felt such joy in seeing these four gay and vigorous creatures living in intimacy with him that nothing else mattered. For Edmond, money was only a means of obtaining the basic possessions of men. He would gladly have spent a fortune on his dogs. This prodigality vexed Rose and Albert, who could not stomach that a half-dog should give to dogs what men often cannot give to other men.

One of Edmond's pleasures was to lie on the lawn and wait until André or Lucien took notice of him. The two of them would approach, playfully nibble him and jump on him. Edmond would catch them by the neck or ears, tumble them over and wrestle with them. Often William, and even the grave Alexander, would join in the fray. These five intertwined, growling, heaving, bounding creatures made a strange picture.

Edmond cared for his four dogs in four ways. He was friends with André and William, but a little in love with Lucien, the setter, and Alexander, the Great Dane. This last one had such short hair that he seemed naked. Edmond always stroked him with reserve. To stroke such a naked animal seemed reprehensible to him. He protected himself from all confusion of feeling. When Alexander, lying on his back, offered the spectacle of his stomach, Edmond would turn away his eyes in embarrassment. Finally, if the dog, standing as tall as a man on his hind legs, placed his paws on Edmond's shoulders and licked him, Edmond's delight was not divorced from shame. He experienced a carnal emotion in seizing and squeezing Alexander's paw, and abstained from this as much as possible. Of them all, it was Alexander that he liked best to take out in his car. Massive and calm, the Great Dane gave the impression of a natural protector.

Lucien, on the other hand, was as inconsistent and frisky as a young girl. He gamboled, capered and yapped; sudden panic would seize him, when he would race trembling to the shelter of his master's arms. At other times, quivering with affection, his brown eyes brimming with adoration, he would approach with a real lover's shyness which stirred our hero to the marrow. He would lie half across Edmond, who could feel his warm body, and, resting his head on his chest, give him melting looks. This was immodesty incarnate: all setters have this habit. But Edmond watched himself too

closely to take it in cold blood. He believed that
Lucien loved him, and reproached himself for the
voluptuous pleasure this idea incurred.

In his relations with William and André, he was
no more ill at ease than any master with any dog.
André, the irrepressible poodle, was an individ-
ualist; egotistical, he shifted for himself, conducted
love affairs with the bitches in the neighborhood,
formed outside friendships, etc. It happened sometimes that he was absent for a whole day and returned in the evening with a light in his eyes which
intrigued Edmond. Once he ran away for three
days and returned in the same good humor. What
had he been up to? Nobody will ever know. André
bore the secret to his grave. If Lucien carried on
like a young girl, André did so like a man.

Lastly, William was the victim of a sort of social
inequality. From the first day he set himself up as
a servant. This modest dog, full of good will, faithful but with an inferior mentality, was well satis-
fied with barking noisily at passers-by and vigilantly
guarding the house. He cared only for Edmond and
his servants. He was the only one who found favor
with Rose, who spoiled him atrociously. As double
proof of his servile nature, he was happiest in the

kitchen, and he soiled or destroyed very little.

The smell of dogs which had formerly choked Edmond was now quite agreeable to him. As he worked in his library, with his dogs lying around him, he would breathe in their sickly clinging odor; a house inhabited by four dogs becomes permeated with their smell, even if they are clean and well cared for. Edmond noted these changes in himself. He attributed them to his age; in growing old one comes to understand others better and learns to love them in all their aspects: a little true affection makes one's nose less sensitive. There was, it is clear, a great deal of wishful thinking in Edmond's reasoning, but it could hardly be otherwise. The elements of his happiness were too abnormal for him to dare to analyze them seriously, even to himself in private. Convinced that he had irrevocably elected to be a man, he admitted only to human sentiments and duped himself in good faith with phrases such as: "One is what one wishes to be. A man's aspirations are the man himself. I want to become a man, I wish it with all my heart; that is enough for me to become one, almost."

In society his taste for dogs passed as a vice, which made him still more interesting. When, on recovering from his despair, he reopened his house, the changes which his guests found there, its canine rulers and Edmond's flourishing appearance, filled them with glee. What an amusing piece of gossip to spread! It canonized him. "Chaillu has provided himself with a real harem of dogs," they said, shaking with laughter. "We knew it would end like that." One dared not think of the saturnalia at Louveciennes. "He has a famous predecessor," declared a scholar. "The Duc de Vendôme, in the eighteenth century, made love with his dogs in just the same way." These good people would have been vastly disappointed had they suspected Edmond's purity! For himself, he lacked nothing, not even love; for, as it once more became fashionable to dine with him, the women, despite his alleged bestiality (or because of it), curried his favors. He had the satisfaction of cuckolding some very fine gentlemen free. One woman said to him during a passionate transport: "Edmond, take me like a bitch!"

Edmond put this down to sensual frenzy and drew no conclusion as to the reason for his successes. Infinitely far from such thoughts, he confidently imagined: "Women like me more and more.

This is irrefutable proof that I am becoming more like a man every day."

Another woman asked him: "Do you love me as much as your dogs?"

"What a question!" he naïvely exclaimed.

At this point a little adventure must be included, a plot woven by an unfortunate husband, out of which Edmond cleverly extricated himself. Edmond loved fancy-dress balls and masked suppers. Surrounded by masks and dominoes, himself disguised, he forgot that he differed from men and became what he knew himself at heart to be: a distinguished wit, capable of brilliant and instructive conversation; a sensitive soul, worthy to experience the subtlest emotions. To one of these balls the husband of one of his mistresses brought a huge dog dressed up as a man and trained to walk for some distance on its hind legs. It was a hound. Its head offered some resemblance to Edmond's, and the dog, got up in a made-to-measure tail coat, stiff shirt, white tie, braided trousers, and a topper held on by elastic, was lamentably comic. Silence fell as the dog and the man arrived. The latter went up to Edmond. "I knew you would be here, so I took the liberty of bringing along a relation of yours."

"Charmed, I'm sure," said Edmond to the dog, as he shook its paw, "but what low company you keep!"

The next morning Edmond and the cuckold fired pistols at each other. This duel served as great publicity for Edmond.

Is it credible that, with the violent and conflicting emotions which ravaged our hero's heart, there could still be room in it for friendship? And yet he had two friends for whom he would have gone through fire: the scholar who had quoted the Duc de Vendôme in his connection, and a retired prefect who dwelt at Louveciennes. These intelligent and cultivated men had not big hearts. They spent two or three evenings at Edmond's house every week, for he was rich and provided good cognac and entertaining conversation. They rendered him the small services customary between friends. As for Edmond, he had flung himself heart and soul into friendship. Anyone who spoke disparagingly of his friends he would have thrown out of his house without hesitation. He read Montaigne with delight and compared that author's feelings for La Boétie with his own for the retired prefect and the scholar. He heaped small gifts on each of them—

books, trinkets. His best evenings were those he
spent with them smoking his pipe, drinking and
arguing in his library. He emerged from these sessions completely happy, having even forgotten his
dogs. "Ah!" he thought. "My true vocation is
friendship, and nothing else. What else *could* one
have with a dog's head? How lucky I am to have
met these two superior, kind, intelligent men, who
are in harmony with me on all important questions
and who catch my slightest meaning!"

Alas, true friendship breaks down all barriers and
establishes complete equality. Edmond, sincere and
simple, fully believed himself the equal of the prefect and the scholar, but they at no time believed
themselves the equals of Edmond, never ceasing to
regard him as a being of an inferior quality. Between themselves they discussed him in a condes-
cending and protective manner. They said: "Poor
old Edmond . . ." and were convinced that they
paid him a great honor in drinking his cognac and
listening to his talk. In selecting them Edmond had
lacked perception. He could have found better.
There are at least fifty people in Paris capable of
rising above the obstacles set by a dog's head.
Eventually he perceived that he was receiving

much less from his friends than he gave them. This
realization plunged him into the deepest gloom.
His awakened mind discerned in their attitude an
imperceptible disdain, an imponderable restraint.
His wounded heart exaggerated this into contempt
and indifference. That was the end of the scholar
and the retired prefect.

As for his dogs, did they not also affect a certain
coldness? There was no precise indication, certainly, but it seemed to Edmond that they no
longer showed him their customary trust and affection. They behaved in the same way as usual, but
his disappointment in friendship compelled him
toward a melancholy and pessimistic attitude. He
was, as we have seen, a sensitive and impressiona-
ble individual, who switched with ease from extreme joy to somber depression. Suddenly his
imagination capsized and everything became black.
This time he discovered that his nature was *incommunicable*. This word constantly cropped up in
his meditations: "I've found it at last; I am of an
incommunicable nature. Nobody understands me
because nobody resembles me, a dog no more than
a man. Incommunicable . . . that is the word. I
shall never find my counterpart: he would have to

be like me, halfway between man and dog." This, he saw, was the reason for his amorous triumphs. His mistresses? A flock of depraved creatures. The pleasures of wealth and the illusion of sentimental success had clouded his critical faculty, but now it was clear once more—clear and desperate. Every woman who had given herself to him belonged to the same category: society women, amoral *bourgeoises* in search of a new sensation. Well, henceforth Edmond would refuse to be nothing but a new sensation. He held short debate with himself: Was he right to be so squeamish? Wouldn't it be more sensible to profit from the depraved curiosity of women? No, no . . . it was unworthy, it was degrading. "Oh, to be a man," he murmured, "a man in spite of everything!" He pronounced this vow without conviction, for he had lost confidence. He groped for something to hold on to.

He retained such an unpleasant memory of his last fit of despair, however, that he sought some distraction. He decided on travel. He would go to Egypt. His mind was so mobile that this project alone was enough to calm him. He had often dreamed of Egypt, the birthplace of Horus, the human god with a falcon's head, and Anubis, the human god with the head of a jackal. On leaving, he gave detailed instructions to Rose and Albert to take great care of the four dogs and never to thwart their desires.

He was away for six months. How had he lived till now without seeing Egypt? In Egypt the past is not dead; nothing divides it from the living present, and it is the very land of dual beings. In Egypt, Anubis is no mere figure, the plastic image of a fictitious monster, but a whole race of statues who hymn the glory of a being almost real, with a man's body and the pointed head of a jackal, to whom dozens of generations have attributed miracles. How pleasant to think that the goddess of love, the Egyptian Venus, Eubastis, bore a cat's head on her seductive woman's body, and that every cat shared something of her divinity! Edmond explored the countryside, visited the ruins and the museums, and bathed in the Nile. Through the Egypt of to-day he pursued the trail of the Egypt of antiquity. He rediscovered hundreds of ambiguous creatures who enchanted him: Hathor, goddess of the desert, who had a cow's head; Upuaut, the wolf-headed god of Lycopolis; Sekhmet, goddess of power, who

had the head of a lioness; Amou, who had the head
of a ram. At Thebes, Opet, the hippopotamus-
goddess, was worshiped and every year there was a
festival dedicated to her which surpassed all others.
At Heliopolis they worshiped Thoth, the god of
intelligence, who had an ibis's head. Was it not
wonderful that Thoth reigned not only over Heliopolis but also over the whole empire: that the
empire in its entirety paid homage to the god of
intelligence, the *psychopompos* Hermes? Edmond
discovered that Ombos and Tentyros had hurled
themselves into frenzied warfare because one of
these two cities had slain the other's sacred croco-
dile. He marveled that in those happy times people
should fight over animals, even hideous ones, and
hated the Romans with all his might for laughing
at this war. This bellicose city of Ombos, in Upper
Egypt, particularly pleased him as having placed
itself under the protection of Set, the repugnant,
the spirit of evil, whose head derived from the ass
and the pig, creatures of the devil indeed. Edmond
would have liked to be a spirit of evil, for no soul
is without romanticism; but he had to admit that
his pretty spaniel's head and his good nature went
ill with a dark legend of treachery and bloodshed.

From the centaurs, the sirens and the sphinx Edmond had finally evolved an ideal of perfection: the human head signified intellect and the animal body strength. He lamented that he was its reverse —with a weak and vulnerable human body and a stupid animal's head. But the gods of Egypt reassured him in their similarity to himself. They offered him proof that not only the intellect but also the divine spirit may dwell in an animal's head. When one is prey to a torment one finds reasons for grief and joy in absurdities. "Of what could I be the symbol?" Edmond asked himself: a futile question. Anubis, with his jackal's head, was the god of death. "With my dog's head I am an earthly symbol," decided Edmond. "My dog's head chains my destiny to the earth." He built for himself a philosophy in which animals were scraps of living earth, emanations of the planet. He took his stand on that passage in Ovid, borrowed from the Egyptians, which deals with the resurrection of humanity after the Flood: "The laborers, on turning up the clods, meet with very many animals, and among them, some just begun at the very moment of their formation, and some they see still imperfect, and as yet destitute of some of their limbs; and often, in the same body, is one part animated, the other part is coarse earth." He imagined Anubis beneath the ground, ruling over the dead, and fancied that he himself was perhaps destined to a similar, posthumous occupation.

Edmond brought back to France dozens of statues of Anubis. "My ancestors!" he cheerfully announced when displaying them to his guests. Egyptology now became his hobby; but he possessed too much money to take more than a dilettante interest in any science.

Despite this, he found great pleasure in his new craze. He dreamed that, had he been born three thousand years earlier, he would have been worshiped in Egypt.

FIVE

W HEN Edmond met Anne at a reception, soon after his return from Egypt, he felt no presentiment; no internal voice cried out: "There goes your destiny!" On the contrary, he believed himself as far from possessing this woman's body as the earth is from striking a planet several million light-years away. "Such women are not for dog-heads," he told himself. He could see Anne's profile ten feet away. When she threw him a look he wished that he could vanish. He loathed himself, longed and feared to be introduced to her, raged at being the only man out of two billions to have a dog's head. If only he could temporarily exchange that head of his for a face, never mind what sort, the vilest, the ugliest, but a face!

Anne was well-bred. She flung a charming smile at Edmond, eyed him as if he were the most seductive of mortals, and talked to him with bewitching courtesy. This did not impress Edmond unduly; he had met other society women. She paid his person a special consideration, looked at him as if he were someone whose opinions were particularly valuable and worthy of her attention. Pure politeness, no doubt, but a spell cast itself over our hero. Like a schoolboy he discussed paintings, literature and music. Anne followed him through these topics and made the correct answers. Edmond gasped in wonder: she shared his tastes! There could be no doubt that Pisanello, Monteverdi and Vauvenargues inspired the same feelings in her as in Edmond. He marveled that such an attractive woman should have such a wealth of mind and spirit. He made subtle and profound remarks. He was delighted with himself and even more with the girl who inspired him in this way. On two or three occasions Anne fixed him with a dreamy eye.

Back at Louveciennes, he thought of Marianne, the first and last woman for whom he had felt real love. "Anne," he said, "is half Marianne. I must expect from her at least half the unhappiness I had from the other." He could not bring himself to imagine Anne's debasing herself with a man with a dog's head. What is strange is that he did not even desire it. This reflection horrified him. A tendency for self-sacrifice is a grave symptom of love. He determined to flee from Anne.

He met her again the next day. Later on she confessed that she had engineered this second meeting. She greeted him with genuine pleasure. Edmond divined charming thoughts behind her wide eyes. He decided to break off their friendship.

"One wouldn't put a dog out in this weather," he said.

Anne's face darkened as if these words had been aimed directly at her. She hastened to speak, to ask Edmond his news, and to compliment him on his elegance. He declared with a snigger: "I'm your own proud and generous bowwow."

Anne's features again clouded with distress.

"Devil take it," thought Edmond, "this is a sensitive woman," and he continued clumsily:

"Don't you think this place smells rather of dogs?"

"Shut up," said Anne, "or I'll start to cry."

After a heavy silence, Edmond found the courage to announce with a sort of timid brutality: "I trust we aren't just going to stare at each other like two china dogs. . . ."

Anne seized his hand and squeezed it. She was indeed crying: a large, round tear slid down her cheek.

Anne was twenty-five: she was a widow and had no parents. A man with a human face could not have desired a more suitable mistress. Tall and well-built, she had that air of gentle dignity, that eminently sane and human beauty that nervous characters delight in. Edmond risked no further jokes about his spaniel's head; he had repelled the Fates as much as lay in his power.

Anne took her seat in Edmond's car with wifely familiarity, and slipped her hand under Edmond's arm. He instantly began to assess her possible motives. She was not a perverse woman. A perverse woman has a vulgar soul and would not weep when a monster made bitter jokes about himself. She was rich, so she could not be after his money. Did she, then, love him? It was incredible. In a voice more soft and tender than Edmond had ever yet heard, she sighed rather than said: "Here at last is he for whom my heart has been waiting!"

Edmond shivered. These amazing words were surely destined from the beginning of time; a page in his life was being turned and happiness was finally to be his lot. Trembling, he took Anne in his arms. He had no idea that a woman could put so much abandon and love into the way she surrendered herself to him. He took her to Louveciennes, where she gave herself so violently, so completely, that he had no further doubts. She loved him, and even in her most frenzied moments preserved a sort of shyness which enchanted Edmond above all. He held in his arms the woman of his dreams, whom he had never thought to possess. "I am saved," he thought in exultation. "Anne loves me as a man is loved. I was right not to despair. I had to have a woman's love to cross over completely to the side of men." He loathed the ridiculous emotions that Henri, Lucien and Alexander had aroused in him. Love dogs? What an idea! With what pathetic substitutes does the heart deceive itself in its thirst for love! "I was like an elderly spinster," he concluded with amusement. "Only old

spinsters really feel the way I did about dogs!" The
thought that he had been tormented by a possible
choice between men and dogs made him shrug his
shoulders. A choice for him? How could he have
entertained such lunacy? He was entirely human.
His dog's head was nothing at all. Anne had pene-
trated beyond his appearance. She had at once
glimpsed the superior man behind the white and
yellow fur. "I am a man," repeated Edmond, "a
normal man. I possess a woman who is neither
venal nor perverted, who loves me for myself, for
my human qualities." He could no longer tolerate
the sight of his dogs. Their smell turned his stomach. He sold all four of them without regret and
had the house disinfected. He broke with a past of
ambiguity and sorrow. He never tired of asking his
mistress: "Do you love me?" like any other lover;
and she never wearied of replying: "I adore you."
Indeed, she behaved like a votary, never leaving
her peculiar lover, ceaselessly touching him, as if
to reassure herself that he wasn't a ghost. She was
submission itself, inventing a thousand little atten-
tions every day. Her love was as the purest water.
It was plain that she had never loved before and
would never love anyone but Edmond. "Here at

last is he for whom my heart has been waiting."
There was no artificiality in these words. They
were the exact truth. Edmond was not accustomed
to this.

One cannot live in constant ecstasy. In his lucid
moments, Edmond thought that a man with a dog's
head did not deserve such felicity and feared the
jealousy of the gods. Yet he had to abandon himself to it; there was nothing equivocal in Anne's
conduct—she was a flaming torch of passion. One
day Edmond, being short of money, asked her for
a hundred thousand francs to buy some likely
shares. She gave them to him on the spot and refused the receipt he offered her. This gesture wiped
away his last reservations. "Anne is the chance of
my lifetime," he decided. "I have met an angel. I
am saved, saved forever."

It was hot. Each morning they awoke naked on
their tousled bed. Their bodies were beautiful, but
Edmond's head was a blot on this charming landscape. It jarred in an intolerable way. He was well
aware of this and hid it under the pillow. Modesty
for him consisted in covering not his loins but his
head. Anne could not understand this feeling. She
would caress Edmond's head, take it between her

hands and, as Edmond formerly did with Henri, look deep into his eyes. It seemed that what she preferred in her lover was precisely this extravagant head which he himself had disowned. "Lay your head on my stomach," she would say. Edmond laid his head on Anne's warm, soft, palpitating stomach, while she closed her eyes and appeared to be overcome with supernatural joy. On other occasions she would lean back, scrutinize Edmond's head and then abruptly smother it with kisses. These demonstrations embarrassed Edmond, who believed that Anne loved him despite his head and not because of it. Anne, who wanted to have Edmond's head constantly under her gaze, innocently thwarted all the attempts he made to conceal it. For example, when he buried his muzzle in Anne's armpit, she would gently pull it out by the scruff of his neck, bring his eyes level with her own and smile at him. In the end, Edmond asked her out of curiosity: "Why do you look at me all the time? Anyone might think you loved me only for my head. That would be too funny!"

"Hush!" whispered Anne mysteriously.

Edmond slid his muzzle between Anne's breasts and languidly licked her neck. Anne murmured endearments: "My beloved, my darling, my sunbeam, my Egyptian god, my Prince Charming."

"Prince Charming" recurred frequently. One day she repeated this expression ten times running.

"I am neither a prince nor charming," said Edmond in embarrassment.

"Yes, yes," replied Anne, "you are my Prince Charming and I adore you."

Rather theatrically, in order to test his mistress, Edmond continued with a forced laugh: "My mother obviously made love with a dog. That's why I have this head. . . ."

Anne clasped his neck in a strangle hold and cried: "If you say such a horrible thing again I'll kill myself."

Edmond's bliss and rapture cannot be described. They were the bliss and rapture of love. He learned to live in intimacy with a woman. Anne had taken charge of the household at Louveciennes, gave the servants their orders, checked the bills, pursued the dust and chose the meals. What joy it was to watch her thus playing the housewife, and to think that it was all for him! Anne's body held no secrets for Edmond. He helped her to dress; he was the witness of his mistress's every act and knew even her smallest thoughts. She lived before his gaze without modesty. She and he were one. To possess a woman in this way was quite a different thing from controlling two mercenary servants. Anne he had not bought. She had given herself to him as one does to a man. She drew no distinction between Edmond's flesh and her own. This last thought had something unbearably exquisite about it. Edmond's flesh was an unfathomed and unique mixture of man and dog. Was it then really lovable? Lovable to the point that a woman had chosen it and desired endless fusion with it? Anne's love promoted Edmond, raised him one grade in the hierarchy of species, naturalized him as a man. When she wound her lovely arms round his furry neck, he had to repress a movement of insane pride. He had indeed something of which to be proud. Had he not, with his dog's head, conquered everything? A superior woman, a beauty, loved him as men are not often loved.

Happiness has not reassuring and tranquil aspects alone. It has also its terrifying ones, which one can perceive better than anyone when one has a dog's head. A dog's head makes one philosophic. Edmond gorged himself with love, with the confused feeling that he was enjoying an incomprehensible godsend which would not last, which must be exploited to the full and which was perhaps founded on a misconception, which one day would explode. When one looks at it coldly, it must be admitted that Anne's love for Edmond was disturbing. Every time he touched her, clasped her in his arms, he thought: "I shall always have had this. This at least they cannot take away from me. I shall have had it."

This lack of confidence in happiness was really poignant.

When Anne called him her "Prince Charming" Edmond always felt a twinge in his heart. It seemed to him too absurd and it was the name Anne took most pleasure in giving him, without the least irony. So far as that is concerned, she never allowed herself to tease him for a moment. Edmond would not have minded had she gently mocked him over his appearance. On the contrary, each time there was any question of his head, Anne assumed a grave air which Edmond judged slightly inhuman.

When he asked her why she loved him, she replied with sibylline intensity: "I love you for what you will become."

Every day she told him: "You must submerge

yourself in my love. There must not remain one shred of bitterness in your heart."

In smothering him with love, she seemed to be fulfilling some sort of sacred duty. Edmond's defeatist spirit dared to suggest to him that Anne had a deranged mind, but how could that be the case? She was too sensitive and reasonable for any suspicion to be seriously cast on her. And yet the idea of Anne's possible insanity fascinated Edmond, or, rather, gave him the vertigo one feels when imagining some catastrophe. With morbid satisfaction he envisaged his despair should his presentiment prove to be well founded. He also argued with himself: "It is I who am mad to think up such things. How could I have got such an idea in my head? Everything about Anne's behavior proves that she is an intelligent, discerning, sensitive woman, and here am I declaring for no particular reason that she is off her head and building up a ludicrous drama. Prince Charming, applied to me, sounds odd, but we all know that love thrives on odd nicknames."

It was in vain: despite himself, at each hour of the day he noticed intangible factors. Trembling, he sensed a slight but inexplicable distress in

126

Anne's voice when she asked him: "Is there still bitterness in your heart?"

Anne put this question twenty times a day. Her insistence alarmed Edmond. Certainly no bitterness remained in his heart, but anxiety established itself in its place. An explanation which brings everything into the light is the sole way to re-establish happiness thus undermined. Anne visibly had no suspicion of the storm that was brewing in her lover. When at last he begged her to tell him frankly and precisely what particular feelings his head awoke in her, she replied without any ado, but as she talked a deadly chill stole through Edmond.

"Your head?" she said. "It's nothing. It doesn't count. It's not your own head. Didn't you know? Every time I look at it, and God knows how often that is, I see your true face barely concealed by your fur. A splendid face, the face of the handsomest young man in the world. The face you are going to recover. Ah, my love, I live only for the day when your fur falls away, when your features resume their rightful place and you become the wonderful prince you should always have been."

Edmond closed his eyes. He experienced what is

so justly termed an internal collapse. It seemed to him that his heart, his liver and all his organs floated loose, and that all his thoughts were tumbling down into heaven knows what dark abyss. "Words of love," he repeated to himself, "words of love, the silly words of passion, nothing more." But his inner consciousness would not be deceived; it knew the truth: Anne was mad. With a great effort, Edmond said in a harsh, vulgar tone: "A Prince Charming, eh?"

"Yes," said Anne, "a Prince Charming. The Prince Charming you really are. . . ."

"No, no," thought Edmond in a fury. "It's impossible. Anne is not mad. She is making fun of me. She is stringing me along, and I, like an imbecile, let myself be strung. Come now, I'll burst out laughing, she will laugh too and my nightmare will be at an end."

Edmond gave vent to a frantic guffaw.

"You laugh," said Anne sadly. "You laugh. . . . You mustn't laugh, sweetheart. What I say is true. Do you want me to tell you your story? Afterwards you'll be convinced."

"That's right," said Edmond in a curious, high-pitched voice. "Tell me my story!"

"Yours is a beautiful story, Edmond. A wonderful, unbelievable and yet true story. When you were born a wicked fairy leaned over your cradle and transformed your baby head into a dog's. She was angry, you understand; she was the only one who had not been invited to your christening. This was her revenge."

"This was her revenge," repeated Edmond ironically.

"Then your parents, the King and the Queen, handed you over in despair to some peasants, who bore you far from your native land and brought you up. You will never recover your true appearance and mount the throne of your fathers until a woman loves you enough to dispel by her affection all the bitterness that the mockery of mankind has stored up in your heart. I am that woman. I can prove it."

"What is this proof?" asked Edmond, who hadn't quite been able to follow.

"The proof is that I suffer when you suffer. When I look at you, I think of all the unkind things that have been said to you, of all the intrigues raised against you, of all the insults, the offenses, the affronts, all the calumnies hurled against

you, my poor, adorable innocent; and my very heart
aches with grief. Even if you were not a Prince
Charming, if you were condemned to have a dog's
head till you die, I believe I should love you just
the same. I should love you for your misfortune.
But God be praised, you are a Prince Charming.
What luck. . . . And I shall be your queen!"

This mixture of sublime love and raving lunacy
overwhelmed Edmond. He did not know what to
think or feel. One moment he loved the mad Anne
more than ever, the next he was frozen with horror.
Blandly, Anne said: "To be your queen, beloved.
. . . That is my destiny. I realized that a long time
ago. Now you can understand my joy at finding
you."

For more than an hour she embroidered this ridiculous tale, adding details, confirming her state-
ments by argument. Like Don Quixote, who talked
wisely and illuminatingly on every subject but
raved like a lunatic when it came to chivalry, Anne,
who loved Pisanello and was passionately addicted
to Vauvenargues, became stark mad where Prince
Charmings were concerned.

Edmond should have rejoiced at Anne's demen-
tia, which deluded her only in so far as he was

concerned; on the contrary, it afflicted him deeply. His honest, Cartesian mind could not permit him to benefit from an aberration. His discovery over Anne froze him as much as if he had suddenly realized that his mistress was a leper. The roles were reversed: it was Edmond's turn to know the loathing he had so often inspired. He spent two cruel days during which this loathing often came close to prevailing over him completely. Anne's beauty and the happiness she had brought him no longer counted for anything. There remained only a crazy woman with whom he had been blindly in love. But the chief reason for his despair was an egotistical one: if Anne was mad, then he was not saved—an appalling disappointment. Anne was his last card. He had staked everything on it. But one cannot win when one has a dog's head. One is doomed to failure. Ah, did you think, my friend, that you could cross just like that to the side of men? It is only real men, endowed with human noses, human eyes, human mouths and human hair who are admitted to the side of men. "Hair," he cried, "I shall never grow hair. Fur, always my fur. It's ghastly. I did not deserve this curse."

What a hurry he had been in to sell Alexander,

and Lucien, and André, and William! He should
have been more cautious, have suspected that for
him happiness would always be precarious and
temporary. William, Alexander, Lucien and André
would have been useful to him now. How could
he have conceived a dislike for those noble beasts
who had never let him down? One must really
adapt oneself to what one is made for. Edmond's
future stretched out before him: he would sink
lower and lower. The dog, the dog, that is what
lay in wait for him. He was broken. He would offer
no further struggle. "A common cur," he cried in
anguish. "That's what will become of me. I was
mad to think I could alter my condition by a step
up the ladder. Raise myself? What a farce! All I
am permitted is to go to the dogs!"

Despite these desperate conclusions, Edmond determined on one final attempt. He decided to make
Anne undergo a cure. The idea that, once cured,
she might no longer love him did not deter him.
By cunning stratagems he persuaded her to go and
spend a year in a psychiatric clinic.

Their parting was heart-rending. Under the at-
tendants' eyes, Anne hugged Edmond to her. She
sobbed and clung to him like a drowning man to a

spar. Her tears matted the fur on Edmond's muzzle. She covered his nose with convulsive little kisses, slid her tongue between his fangs, clutched at his ears. As they dragged her off to her room, she cried: "Set me free soon!"

In this tragic moment Edmond could not refrain from a feeling of pride. "There goes somebody who is suffering because of me," he told himself. "At least I have made a woman weep."

SIX

I SHALL not undertake to describe in detail how, in one year, Edmond lost all his property. The clinic was very expensive. He summoned doctors from Vienna and New York, who robbed him of several million francs. An unfortunate deal on the Stock Exchange took the remainder. He had to sell Louveciennes and the car. To reconstruct his fortune, Edmond had but to borrow a little—he did not lack credit—and place it where it would bear fruit. He was a clever enough speculator for that: but a bewitching voice, at once sweet and bitter, murmured in his ear that it is all one to be rich or

poor when one has a muzzle covered with yellow
and white fur. His existence seemed to him to be
a series of oscillations increasing in force between
dog and man. Edmond had never been so close to
men as during the time of Anne. He could easily
picture where the pendulum would now drag him,
and he did not care. Anne's lunacy marked the end
of a cycle.

Something which belonged to the human side
of Edmond's nature snapped. The spirit of enterprise had deserted him, as also the strictly human
ambition of happiness.

This change was surprising in a being who had
always shown himself to be courageous, but it must
not be forgotten that Edmond was afflicted with an
extreme sensibility, which tossed him endlessly between joy and despondency. Crushed once again,
he could not manage to raise himself. Perhaps it
was also necessary that a sharp division should take
place in his mind and that he should choose one
or the other of the two natures of which he was
composed. A terrible choice because it was not preordained and had not depended upon Edmond. An
unforeseen event, the madness of the woman who
loved him, had determined this final stage. An un-

foreseen event? Is that certain? Who but a mad
woman could have fallen in love with Edmond?
Was not Edmond destined for all time, as he himself had said, to go "to the dogs"?

By the end of this cruel year, which he spent in
paying the clinic, the doctors, and losing on the
Stock Exchange, his torpor became so great that he
did not even take the trouble to think things out.
He fled from conversation, maintained a moody
silence, answered beside the point and laconically.
He accepted all things with the same indifference.
"Fate has placed a collar round my neck," he
thought. "It holds me on a leash. I have always
worn this collar and this leash. Formerly I was
unaware of them. Today I realize their existence.
That is the only difference." It would seem unlikely
that such a realization could be strong enough to
break a character forever. And yet this is what happened. Within a year, the idea of the invisible collar and leash established itself in Edmond's mind
and became an indisputable conviction. This led
to renunciation, and renunciation has an hypnotic
quality. Edmond felt the shock of all this to the
very depths of his dual being. His existence had
been a succession of false victories and true set-

backs. When he went back fearfully over his past, a sickening odor of absurdity floated up from this well of years. His dog's head was an agent of corruption. Everything was poisoned by its touch. What more dazzling proof of this could there be than his last adventure? There is nothing finer than a great love shared, nothing begets more happiness for men. For men, yes, men with human heads. A man with a dog's head draws from the purest source of happiness nothing but a grief more acrid than those he has known before.

Edmond had no faith; the hope of a better world did not sustain him in any way. In moments of burlesque bitterness, he pictured himself dead, among the Blessed in Paradise, with his spaniel's head in an aureole of light on top of an immaculate white robe, and agreed that after all it was preferable that there should be no Beyond. Without faith, life with a dog's head is hard. Had he been logical to the end, Edmond would doubtless have committed suicide: but suicide requires some trace of the spirit of enterprise, and he had become too filled with lassitude to undertake to kill himself. Besides there dwelt in him an obscure spirit of preservation of which he had been unaware in the days when he aspired to identify himself with men. Then he was fired by generosity; like men, he counted life as a small thing. Today, if nothing else had caused him alarm, this egotistical sentiment which ruled heavily and darkly in his stomach, according to which his flesh was something important and to be preserved at all costs, would most certainly have plunged him into veritable terror at the imminence of death.

Without any preparation, he casually announced to Rose and Albert that he had no more money. This dismissal, so out of keeping with general usage, flabbergasted his two faithful servants and filled them with a quite legitimate anger. They did not scruple to steal several trinkets and some linen. One does not let oneself be ruined like that without giving due warning. When Edmond had signed certificates to proclaim that Rose was the most honest of *cordons bleus* and Albert the most refined of butlers, Albert said with an irony which did not escape Rose: "Monsieur needn't worry. He can always get a job as a circus clown."

Rose, stimulated by this remark, capped it: "And in the zoo Monsieur can get as many bones as he likes."

Albert, adorned in a bowler and a black overcoat,
and Rose, surmounted by a hat with a green veil
and enveloped in a red cloak, departed, each carrying a suitcase. Edmond couldn't deny a certain
sadness as he watched their silhouettes diminish.
With them went the last of what had constituted
the best in his life. But had there ever been a "best"
in his life? No! Merely periods of lucidity and
periods of blindness.

The year devoted to Anne's sojourn in the psychiatric clinic finally elapsed, in the midst of these
sorrows. It would be madness to think that Edmond
had become totally brutish. He could on occasion
sustain a conversation: his terror of reasoning was
not perceptible to everyone. He felt—how can it be
explained?—that, to the end of his days, which he
hoped was far distant, he would know when necessary how to discuss Bergson's philosophy or talk
prettily of Watteau's painting, but that he would
take less and less pleasure in it.

Anne left the clinic as mad as she went in.

"My God," she cried on seeing Edmond once
more, "have you still got your dog's head? Haven't
I suffered enough, then? I shall love you all the
more."

These words blazed a trail straight to the new Edmond's benumbed heart. He judged that a man with a dog's head should consider himself very lucky to be loved by a pretty woman, even if she were slightly mad. Why hadn't he thought of this sooner? Alas, a year earlier, he had loved Anne with the heart of a man. He would not have desired such a compromise. The old hope flickered once more, but feebly. Anne, crazy as she was, could still be a safety-belt. Yet, truth to tell, Edmond hardly believed this. Right now he felt himself to be too far "gone to the dogs" to be able to climb back; but, through a singular point of honor, he wished to leave Fate no margin which might make it possible to say that he had not tried everything, and more, to be a man. At bottom, it was a characteristic act of despair which he set himself to accomplish.

"I am ruined," he told Anne. "I haven't a penny. Will you marry me all the same?"

"With all my heart," she said. "Let's get married at once and we'll never leave each other again."

In marrying this woman whom he no longer loved, and whose love he knew to be ineffectual, Edmond found a sweetness which surprised him;

but when he had signed his name in the town hall's register and heard the embarrassed congratulations of the mayor, he understood that he had taken a futile step which, like all his actions, was absurd; that nothing good could ever be born of a union between a lunatic and a monster. What problems for a being who abandons himself to Fate!

Anne's fortune was much smaller than had been believed. It only just allowed the couple to install themselves in the Hôtel de la Garonne and see what turned up, as the saying goes.

"Well, here you are again, M'sieu Edmond!" said the hotel proprietor. "Whoever would have thought you would be spending your honeymoon at the Hôtel de la Garonne? Money doesn't bring happiness. You have a beautiful wife who loves you, you have your whole life ahead of you, you've got right out of the hole you were in. No more dog stories for you! You've no more reason to envy anybody."

At the end of two months Edmond by chance stumbled on a post as gamekeeper in the Loiret. This job, which he has held now for three years, satisfies him. It is a job halfway between man and dog, and decidedly closer to dogs than men. Each morning Edmond imprisons his calves in leggings

and dons a cloth jacket which buttons up to his
chin. His spaniel's head, emerging from his garb
and outlined against the green landscape, appears
somewhat less bizarre. Edmond feels at peace and
even enjoys moving through a sylvan décor. He
owns two dogs, rather ugly spaniels, which resem-
ble him. It was probably preordained that he should
one day have dogs in his own image. These animals
in no wise take advantage of this. He leads them a
fairly hard life, and they bear him an affection to
which he is not so responsive as he would have
been five years earlier. Waiving his principles, Edmond has not given his dogs human names. The
male is called Sultan and the female Juno, following the purest tradition.

As the months have passed by, Edmond has begun to forget human ways. For example, he laps
instead of drinking, guzzles from his plate, gnaws
bones interminably, and licks the gravy clinging to
his chops. When he catches a fly in his mouth,
Anne claps her hands with delight and cries: "Got
him!"

A second Edmond, who remains human and
hovers above the other, observes these habits with
curiosity, sorrowing and rejoicing over them at the

same time. But the vision of this second Edmond is growing increasingly dim. Soon it will vanish completely. Now that our hero has chosen his side, or, rather, that something within him has chosen his side for him, it is much easier and in a sense more agreeable to slide down toward dogs rather than climb up toward men.

Rising before daybreak, he wanders over the hills and dales of his employers. He runs, jumps, shouts, goes down on the turf and noses out the tracks of game. His sense of smell has become so acute that he discovers something exquisite in the most repulsive odor. Formerly so *soigné*, he now neglects himself and takes pleasure in his own stench. His muzzle hanging down his chest, he sniffs himself deeply, in ecstasy. The eau de Cologne and perfumes which were once his passion make him sneeze. He smells like a dog. He is devoured by fleas; rabbits scamper away when the wind carries his scent to them.

Olfactory sensations constitute the most important part of Edmond's life. They rule his appetites, his dislikes and his ecstasies, for it is in fact an ecstasy which fills him when he brushes by a tree against which his dogs have lifted their legs: a hot rush descends to his stomach, a thrill runs up his spine and he in turn has to relieve himself. Game fills him with a fury which he can no longer control. He flings himself with howls on the trail of hares and snatches the creatures from Sultan's mouth to cram them, still palpitating, between his own jaws. He no longer reads, not even the newspaper, and hardly even speaks. His syntax has become clumsy: he now often expresses himself in savage onomatopoeia. In the grip of anger he begins to bark. During his night rounds, he chases poachers with cries which fall somewhere between barking and speech.

Anne does nothing to combat the brutalization of her husband. She does not seem to suffer from it, or even to notice it. The flames of passion still blaze in her eyes. She looks at Edmond with magnificent eyes and follows his gestures with tender solicitude. She has lost none of her beauty. Rustic tatters have replaced her gowns, that is all. It cannot be claimed that she keeps her little house very clean. Edmond's habits have left their mark on her. By a miracle of love, she has gone to the dogs in her own way. She addresses Edmond in his semi-canine language, serves up and shares with him his foul stews, is amused to see him quarreling with Sultan and Juno over their dog's dinner. The game-keeper's cottage is a kennel swarming with vermin, and ruled by unspeakable smells. Anne knows nothing of cleaning dishes or washing clothes, and as nobody minds, it is better that way. To summon Edmond she gives an affectionate whistle, to which he comes running. The look he gives his wife, who has just recalled herself to his memory in this man-ner, is the very look of a dog who "only lacks the power to talk." It thrills Anne to the depths of her soul.

"Din-dins," she says, pressing Edmond to her and kissing him on the neck. "Food. Yum-yum. A lovely soup. Come and eat."

At night, Edmond dreams the dreams of a fright-ened, beaten or triumphant dog. He utters little yaps in his sleep. This wakes Anne, and she ten-derly gazes at him. She encourages his most dis-gusting whims. It is a long time since Sultan and Juno first came to sleep with Edmond in his bed, and now they even mate in his presence. If a bitch in heat passes near by, Edmond's distracted and trembling air does not even sadden his wife. Her passion for him is so strong and she finds herself so happy simply to be his wife, to see and touch him, that she no longer takes herself into account, so to speak. Only a madwoman can love in such a manner. For his part, as Edmond slowly became transformed, a new love for Anne was born in him, a mixture of faithful affection and violent desire, which fits in very well with his increasing taste for dogs; for by now he constrains himself no longer and pursues males and females with the same ardor. This equal attraction toward either sex deserves to be pointed out: it is completely animal.

What a topic of conversation such a gamekeeper provides for a little village in the Loiret! Edmond is hated, feared and spied on. At the village inn his latest act is discussed with grave noddings of the head. The local poachers, who are terrified of him, heap fuel on the fire; for them the truth does not seem staggering enough. Their imaginations soar. They claim that it is the height of folly to entrust firearms to a monster who wanders baying through the forest. Children are no longer allowed to play in the streets after sundown. Fortunately, crime is almost unknown in the district; otherwise it would certainly be laid at Edmond's doorstep. Everyone knows that he frequently whips his dogs, and that the doleful cries of these wretched beasts give him keen pleasure.

"Poor brutes!" they say. "It's a hell of a life with a master like that!"

"Oh come, don't take on so! He may beat them, but he knows how to cheer them up afterwards."

In short, the village lives in an atmosphere of terror and scandal. They never openly laugh about Edmond. The most moderate demand his internment in an asylum. One day someone will shoot him. Anne also has to face this ostracism. They have nicknamed her "Loopy Anne." Dirty, in rags, with matted hair, she recaptures her old tone when she goes shopping.

"Will you be so good," she says to the baker's wife, "as to let me have a three-pound loaf? I suppose you haven't by chance any cakes?"

This rather precious phraseology, pronounced with a superior accent, sends the tradespeople into fits of laughter. Anne never notices this, any more than she notices when people turn away their heads and hold their noses as she passes. She smiles kindly at the children who giggle at her. Certain tradesmen have rudely forbidden her to enter their shops. Her head and her heart are full of Edmond and see nothing but him. If he should die, she wouldn't survive him by so much as an hour. She no longer wants him transformed into a Prince Charming. On the contrary, were this miracle to be accomplished, she would be most disappointed. Covered with fleas, clothed in tatters, living in a filthy den and betrayed with dogs, she has never been so happy. It is interesting to note that she is three months' pregnant.